## "We need to talk—
## *really* talk."

"No sparring, no fighting," Sam insisted. "Just two neighbors trying to resolve a little dispute in a friendly way. Have dinner with me tonight, Lucky."

As Lucky listened to the wonderful deep cadence of Sam's voice flowing over the line, it never once crossed her mind to refuse him. There were too many issues still unresolved between them—and, for her, business was the least of them.

"If tonight's bad—"

"No, tonight's fine. Pick me up at eight."

As Lucky hung up the phone, she was already figuring out what to wear—her lacy teddy, that red silk dress that had been hanging in the back of the closet for ages.... It was just a friendly dinner, she reminded herself firmly. Sam was *not* planning a seduction.

*Sure*, said a tiny inner voice. That's exactly what the Trojans thought when they accepted that big wooden horse....

**Laurien Berenson** took a little longer than usual to complete *Lucky in Love*, her first Temptation and her eighth published novel. The delay was due to a litter of poodle puppies born *very* prematurely, necessitating round-the-clock feedings. Always one to find the humor in any situation, Laurien laughs and says, "It was just like having another baby!"

Laurien lives in Connecticut with her husband, Bruce, her three-year-old son, Chase . . . and five miniature poodles!

# Lucky in Love
## LAURIEN BERENSON

# *Harlequin Books*

TORONTO • NEW YORK • LONDON
AMSTERDAM • PARIS • SYDNEY • HAMBURG
STOCKHOLM • ATHENS • TOKYO • MILAN

For the gang at Halcyon—
Mark, Danny, Mary Ellen and Penny.
The very best at what they do.

FORTY YEARS OF
Romance

Published June 1989

ISBN 0-373-25355-9

# 1

"I DON'T CARE what you say, I am not riding on the back of any pig!" Lucky Vanderholden glared in outrage at the advertising rep who handled her account. "And that's final!"

"But Lucky, just think about it for a moment." Ed Wharton's voice was soft and cajoling. "This could be just the hook that you need. It'll grab people's attention, bring customers in by the dozens."

There was nothing ladylike about Lucky's answering snort. "Don't be ridiculous, Ed. People are looking for value these days, a good car for a good price—not someone parading around on the back of a pig."

"I don't know, Lucky. That pig idea worked wonders for Loonie Louie over in Norristown."

"Loonie Louie has a lot full of junkers, and he sells half of them for below cost," Lucky pointed out. "I don't."

Ed shrugged. "In the minds of the public a used car's a used car—until you do something to set your business apart. Like Louie did. Now he's got more customers than he can handle." Ed paused to let that sink in. "Customers you could use, Lucky."

Lucky stood and walked out from behind the desk in her office. She crossed the small room and paused before the picture window that overlooked a parking lot full of gleaming used cars. At least Ed was right about one thing, she mused. She *could* use the customers. Lucky's Late-Model Lovelies was carrying far too heavy an inventory.

These past few months, sales had been unusually slow. She'd blamed the slump on a generally sluggish economy. After all, hers wasn't the only business in town that was languishing. Still, the fact remained that something had to be done. Maybe a snappier advertising campaign was what she needed to get things going again.

Lucky nodded to herself as she turned back to Ed who was waiting in the chair beside her desk. "Maybe we should consider taking some spots on local TV," she said slowly.

"That's the spirit!" Ed leaped to his feet. "You won't regret this, believe me—"

"Ed?" The quelling tone in her voice stopped his rush of enthusiasm. "I said I'd look into some new advertising. I didn't say anything about riding a pig."

"Sure, Lucky." Ed flashed an expansive smile. "Anything you say."

After he had gone, Lucky returned to her desk and pulled the ledger out of a side drawer. Opening the thick book, she flipped through its pages. As she came to the entries for the last six months, her hand slowed, then stopped entirely. No doubt about it, the debits outweighed the credits by a large margin. Unless business turned around soon, Lucky's Lovelies was going to be in serious trouble.

The dulcet tones of a deep, melodious horn floated through the summer air and in the open door to Lucky's office. A customer arriving? She glanced up hopefully, just in time to see a maroon and silver Rolls Royce glide past the entrance to her lot and turn into the one next door.

She should have known. Lucky sent a fleeting frown in the direction of Donahue Motors, the impeccable establishment whose lot bordered hers. The dealership specialized in luxury cars—BMWs, Mercedes Benzes and Rolls Royces. Though it had only been open a short while, to all appearances, business was booming.

Patrons came and went at all hours of the day. The stock displayed in the huge, glass-fronted showroom across from her office turned over regularly. And when she walked to the far end of her lot, Lucky was able to see the open bays of the gleaming garage. Inside an army of mechanics clad in burgundy jumpsuits with names like Fritz and Gunter stenciled on the pockets, worked on the spotless engines of spotless cars. From start to finish, the operation was impressive.

If she'd had any yearnings in that direction herself, she would have found her neighbor's display enormously depressing. But fortunately she never had.

No, she was more than satisfied with her used cars—each one different and possessing a history all its own. She was happy with her medium-sized lot, which boasted no showroom at all, but was level and newly paved. And she was thrilled with the services of her mechanic, Clem Greeley, who could fix anything on wheels, but wouldn't have been caught dead in a burgundy jumpsuit.

Besides, Donahue Motors wasn't without problems of its own. The day after Sam Donahue purchased the adjoining lot, he'd installed a six-foot-high fence, topped with a strand of electrical wire. It was posted liberally with No Trespassing signs, and at night two large Doberman pinschers roamed at will.

Obviously nobody was meant to touch those shiny cars except those who had the means to pay for them, Lucky mused. How different that was from her own lot where the customers roamed at will—everyone from sixteen-year-old boys who browsed with wide-eyed interest to empty-nesters looking to trade in the family station wagon for something smaller. It was her policy to welcome everybody, right down to the smallest, sticky-fingered child, with the same warmth and courtesy.

Of course, Lucky thought with a wry tilt to her mouth, these days there wasn't much welcoming being done. She might not agree with Donahue's hands-off policy, but she certainly couldn't argue with his results. Why, in only six months, he'd already succeeded in ...

Lucky frowned suddenly as her own thoughts brought her up short. Six months, now why did that number ring a bell? Gazing down at the ledger, she began to turn back through its pages until she came to January, the month that Donahue Motors had opened beside her.

Sales had been slow, but that wasn't unusual for the time of year. In eastern Pennsylvania, winter months could be cold and blustery and this year had been no exception. By March, the worst of the chilly weather had gone, but the lack of customers remained.

Still, Lucky recalled, she hadn't started to worry until April when the spring rush she'd anticipated had never materialized. By May, her inventory was at an all-time high, and now, in June, nothing much seemed to be happening to counteract that.

There was no doubt about it, Lucky mused. After five years of gratifying, if not stupendous success, her problems had definitely begun when Donahue Motors had opened for business. The question was, why?

Pushing a raft of jumbled papers out of the way, Lucky leaned her elbow on the desk and rested her chin in her hand. Maybe it had something to do with that high, forbidding fence. Though the open access to her lot hadn't really changed, she could see how some people might have gotten confused by the new setup. And even those who weren't confused might have been intimidated. After all, her brand of customers liked to meander through the lot checking out the bargains, then haggling for the best price. They were just the sort of people who would find the display of conspicuous consumption next door rather off-putting.

Perhaps Lucky's Lovelies was also suffering from its close proximity to such an obviously pricey establishment. After all, anyone coming from town had to drive past Donahue Motors on their way to her lot. Who knew what went through their minds when they saw all that finery? One thing was certain, it didn't bring to mind visions of getting a good deal on a secondhand car!

A cooling breeze drifted in through the open doorway, and Lucky lifted her face to it gratefully as she pondered the problem before her.

She'd met Sam Donahue, of course, first when he moved in, and then several times since. As neighbors, it was inevitable that they run into each other, but so far their meetings had been just that—quick run-ins that offered time for little more than a bit of polite conversation.

From what she'd seen of the man, Lucky had been impressed. Though not overly tall, he was well built. His hair was thick and straight, and every bit as dark as hers was blond. His eyes were gray and disarmingly direct. He was not, she suspected, a man who would miss much.

Nor, she'd decided at their first meeting, was he the kind of man who would be happy to coast on the strength of his good looks alone. There was a definite air of intelligence about him and a half-cynical twist to his mouth that spoke volumes about his view of the world.

All in all she'd found him intriguing. And when, after their first meeting, he'd found no reason to follow up their acquaintance, she'd considered that her loss. But then, by the age of thirty, Lucky had learned to be philosophical about such things. She'd been dating long enough to know that attraction wasn't always equally shared. And if Sam had felt none of the pulse-quickening awareness that she had, well then, perhaps that was his loss, too.

With a small sigh, Lucky shook her head. There was nothing she could do about any of that now. Far more pressing was the matter of finding a way to blunt the effect that Donahue Motors was having on her business. There had to be something she could do.

It was ten long minutes before Lucky realized the answer to her problem, and when she did, it was so elementary she was amazed she hadn't thought of it sooner. Obviously the only solution was to fight fire with fire. So, Donahue's Rolls Royces were making her used cars look shabby by comparison. Then rather than trying to avoid the comparison, perhaps she'd be better off playing it up for all it was worth.

Reaching across the clutter on her desk, Lucky plucked up the receiver on her phone and dialed Ed. All of a sudden she knew what her new advertising slogan was going to be, and she wasn't going to have to ride around on the back of any pig, either!

SAM DONAHUE SAT behind the large oak desk in his plushly carpeted office. The blotter before him was empty, the phone silent. Beneath the slim lines of his Italian suit, his shoulders were squared, his posture rigid. He was ready, thought Sam, but for what?

The room was cool and quiet, the steady hum of the air conditioner blocking out all noise from outside. Through a side window he could see an older couple in the lot talking to one of his salesmen.

Briefly he debated getting up and walking out for a quick look around the showroom, then decided against it. Everything was running smoothly, he was sure of it. After all, why shouldn't it be? He'd devoted the last eighteen months of his life to making Donahue Motors a success, and if the figures on the balance sheet were any indication, his hard work was beginning to pay off.

The business was established now and fast on its way to becoming the biggest foreign-car dealership in eastern Pennsylvania. And why not? Sam mused. After ten years in the business working for others, he'd known exactly what was needed when it was time to strike out on his own.

His first decision had been to pick the small town of Cloverdale as his base of operations. It had offered not only proximity to Philadelphia and the toney Main Line, but also favorable zoning and land that could be had at a reasonably affordable price. Once the lot had been acquired, he'd gone about setting up the type of sales and service establishment that most foreign-car owners only dreamed of.

Sam had decided a long time ago that anyone who invested the kind of money that his cars sold for was entitled to top-notch service, and he was determined to see that they got it. He'd imported the best mechanics he could get from the home plant in Germany, then hired a team of salesmen who were as committed to hard work as he was himself.

At Donahue Motors, no mechanic ever muttered about balky gizmos or air conditioners that couldn't be fixed. The salesmen never declared a model or color unavailable. If a customer wanted something, he got it—even if Sam had to scour the entire east coast from Maine to Florida to make that promise come true.

It hadn't taken long for word to spread that Sam Donahue not only had the latest, most popular models in stock, but that he also stood unequivocally behind every car he sold. Donahue Motors was a revelation to foreign-car buyers who were used to being treated as though the dealer was doing them a favor simply by putting their name on the bottom of a long waiting list. And as the books showed, the customers responded accordingly.

Getting the business up and running had been hard work. For eighteen months there'd been no time in his life for anything else. Not that he begrudged the effort it had taken. To the contrary, Sam had found it exhilarating. He loved the challenge and the commitment of giving all he had, even though this was the venture that could make or break him.

He'd given himself a year to start breaking even, and he'd passed that goal in the first three months. He should have been thrilled by how well things were going. So why, instead, was he feeling this vague dissatisfaction, this nagging feeling that there should be something more?

There was a hurried knock on his office door as it opened to admit Joe Saks, one of his senior salesmen. "Hey boss, I think you better see this!"

"What?" Sam looked up, distracted.

"An ad on TV." Joe was waving to hurry him out of his chair. "Come on, you're going to miss it."

Frowning, Sam quickly followed the salesman down the corridor and into the waiting room next to the garage. The television on the far wall was tuned to one of the local stations, and he was just in time to see the last few seconds of a commercial.

A trim woman with curly blond hair was standing in the middle of a parking lot filled with cars of all makes and models. Sam noted with distaste that many had had their prices written across their windshields with a bar of soap. Then he focused on what the woman was saying.

"Remember," she announced with a broad smile. "Those high-priced cars are fine for people who have money to burn."

Sam's eyes narrowed as the camera pulled back then panned another lot filled with Mercedeses, BMWs...*his lot!* he realized with a start. He growled something inaudible under his breath.

Then the camera focused on the woman once more, this time pulling in tight for a close-up of her face. "But at Lucky's Late-Model Lovelies," she continued, "we offer quality merchandise at a *fair* price. Come on down and give us a look. You won't be disappointed."

Again the camera pulled away, this time displaying the lot filled with used cars as the woman said in a voice-over, "Remember, we're Lucky's Lovelies, the Rolls Royce of the used-car business, where you don't have to spend a fortune to drive away feeling like a king."

"I'll be damned," Sam muttered as the image faded away and was replaced by that of a manic-looking game show host.

"I thought you'd be interested," said Joe. "This is the first one I've seen, but a couple of the guys said the station's been running the ad all week."

*All week?* Sam's voice was a controlled roar. "How dare she pull a stunt like that?"

"You know how it is on these local stations, they'll let a person do just about anything. Why, did you know there's a guy over in Norristown who did an entire commercial from the back of a pig? I hear he couldn't sit down for three days . . ."

Sam swung around with an angry glare, and Joe's voice trailed away. "Well," he amended with a shrug, "I was just thinking that maybe we ought to be grateful she didn't do anything truly outlandish."

"You mean like driving a herd of buffalo through the showroom?" Sam inquired archly. "Believe me, as far as I'm concerned, what that woman did do is outlandish enough. Among other things, she implied that our cars sell for a king's ransom."

Joe cleared his throat softly. "If you don't mind my saying so, Mr. Donahue, they—" One look at the expression on Sam's face was enough to make Joe reconsider the wisdom of what he'd been about to say.

"They what?"

"Are worth every penny the customer pays. Yes indeed, they sure are."

To Joe's surprise, Sam's expression lightened. "That's what I thought you were going to say." Unexpectedly, Sam winked then turned and strode from the room.

Looking at his boss's departing back, Joe shook his head. The man never ceased to surprise him. One thing was sure though, he wouldn't want to be in Lucky Vanderholden's shoes right now!

BACK IN HIS OFFICE Sam took a few minutes to compose himself and plan a line of attack. It would not do at all to go about this thing half-cocked. Obviously, the woman had already invested time and money in the television spots. Convincing her to remove them was going to take some doing. But however difficult, Lucky Vanderholden had to be made to see that she could not get away with building up her business at his expense. He simply would not allow it!

Despite the air conditioner, all at once the room felt surprisingly warm. Sam yanked off his jacket, then tossed it carelessly over the back of a chair. He reached up to loosen his tie and pull it free.

Abruptly Sam grinned, his earlier boredom gone. There was nothing like a challenge to get his juices up and running. Leaning against the edge of his desk, he concentrated on remembering everything he knew about his neighbor. The image of the slim young woman he'd just seen on the television flashed through his mind. She was tall, he recalled, almost his height, with golden blond curls that framed her face like a halo of light.

She had presence, Sam mused. The face of a gamine, the posture of a queen. Creamy skin and gold-tipped lashes that matched her hair. Her eyes were dark, a deep, melting shade of brown that he'd noticed immediately.

As they shook hands, she'd held his gaze without pulling away. He liked that. She was, he'd decided, a woman who could hold her own in almost any company, including his.

With a small smile, Sam remembered the quick shaft of attraction he'd felt at their meeting. It was a pity he'd been too busy to follow up on it at the time. Now it was too late. That commercial of hers had seen to that.

Oh well. Sam sighed softly. Some things just couldn't be helped.

LUCKY WAS TALKING on the phone when Sam Donahue appeared in the doorway to her office.

"Yes, Ed," she said, trapping the receiver between her head and her shoulder and motioning for him to come in. "I know, Ed, so far the response has been great."

Sam snorted softly under his breath at the offhand reception. No wonder the woman was having to resort to such underhanded tactics to bring in customers. If this was the way she treated all her visitors, he wasn't surprised at her lack of success.

Striding forcefully into the small room, Sam debated taking a seat. The dichotomy between his large frame and the rickety looking wooden chair—the only seating the room offered—appeared too great. He gave up on the idea and stood instead.

"Yes, Ed, I know," Lucky said impatiently as the advertising rep rambled on and on about the success of her new campaign.

She shot a wary look at her visitor out of the corner of her eye. Though she hadn't dwelt on the possibility, she'd known from the moment she'd seen the finished commercials that he would come. So now that he was here, why did she feel so unprepared?

He attracted her, Lucky thought. That put her at a disadvantage, and she sensed he was a man who would make use of another's weakness. The most important thing was for her to put them on an equal footing—right from the start.

"Look, Ed." Lucky's fingers hovered above the cut-off button. "Something's come up. Now isn't a good time to discuss this. I'll have to call you back, okay?"

Without waiting for his reply, Lucky hung up. Taking a deep breath, she gazed up at Sam with a bright smile. "Mr. Donahue, how nice to see you again. What terrible neighbors we make. It's been how long now . . . ?"

Without thinking Sam returned the smile. He regretted the impulse immediately. "A while," he said vaguely. She didn't need to know that his memory was much better than that. "I drove by one morning when you were out in front trying to interest a little old lady in a red Corvette."

"Ah yes." Lucky leaned back in her chair. "Mrs. Obermann. You honked your horn and waved."

"I was in a hurry," he said. To his surprise, the statement sounded defensive. Even more surprising was the urge to shift uncomfortably on his feet. Automatically he willed himself to stand still.

Damn it, he thought. *He* was the one who held the power position in the room. So why didn't she seem to know that?

"I'm sure you were," said Lucky. "From here it looks as though the luxury-car business is booming."

"It is." Sam's voice was clipped. It was time to take control. "Did she buy the car?"

Lucky saw the subtle shift in his stance, the hardening in the line of his mouth and immediately knew their portent. Instinctively she moved to counteract it.

"Who?"

Sam frowned. For the second time, he'd underestimated her. "Mrs. Obermann. Did she buy the red Corvette?"

"Alas, no." Lucky sighed, her senses honed to match his. They both knew the purpose of his visit, but if he wanted to think he was lulling her into a false feeling of security with small talk, she'd be more than happy to oblige him.

"She didn't think the car suited her image." Lucky allowed a soft chuckle at the memory. "She went for the black Trans Am, instead."

"Oh." Sam was momentarily nonplussed, whether by the story itself or by the sweet sound of her laughter, he wasn't quite sure. Clearly it was time to get down to the business at hand.

"Look," he said firmly. "I'm afraid I haven't come to pay a social call. I want to discuss those commercials you're running on local TV."

"Yes?" Lucky bit her lip and declined to comment further. She'd known the boom would have to fall sooner or later. Well, here it came.

"You filmed those ads like that on purpose."

With effort, Lucky managed a complacent smile. "They could hardly have gotten on the air by accident."

Sam had told himself he'd keep a rein on his temper, but that was before he realized just how much her coolness would incite him. "That's not what I mean, and you know it!"

One finely arched eyebrow rose. "Oh?"

"In the first place," Sam began, "you're using pictures of my lot without my permission."

"Are you so sure it's your lot?"

"Well of course—"

Lucky took pride in knowing that her upward gaze was considerably calmer than it had a right to be. "Did you see your showroom or any of your signs?"

"No, but—"

"Were any of your personnel featured in the footage?"

"Not that I recall, but—"

Lucky smiled coolly. "Then how can you be so sure that it's *your* lot? If you don't mind my saying so, you don't have the only foreign-car dealership in Pennsylvania."

"Of course not," Sam conceded. "But that doesn't change the fact that I'd recognize my own layout and my own cars."

"No," Lucky said slowly, "but it does change the fact of what you could or couldn't prove."

For a moment there was silence as Lucky paused to let that sink in. "Anything else?"

"Yes there's something else!" Sam thundered. Just the tone of his voice would have been enough to make his employees snap to attention. So why didn't *she* seem concerned in the least? "Those ads of yours imply that only rich people can afford to buy my cars."

"Well?"

Sam frowned. "Well, what?"

"That's true, isn't it?"

"Of course not," he growled. "Anyone can patronize Donahue Motors—"

"As long as they're willing to mortgage their house to put up a down payment."

"Now see here." Sam's patience was nearing an end. "I didn't come over here to argue with you about finances. I came because those new commercials of yours are detrimental to my business, and I want you to put a stop to them."

"I'm afraid that's impossible." Lucky tried a conciliatory tone. She'd much rather have been friends with this man than enemies. Too bad it simply wasn't meant to be.

"Those ads are the best thing that's happened to Lucky's Lovelies in the past six months. I'm sorry that you don't like them, but I'm afraid I can't afford to jettison a successful advertising campaign simply to suit your personal whims."

Sam cleared his throat. The sound rumbled through the room like a menacing growl. "You're not the only one who has business interests to protect," he said. "If you persist in running those ads, then I'm afraid I have to take certain steps."

Lucky straightened in her chair. "What steps?"

Sam shrugged. "You know what they say. All's fair in love and war."

Abruptly Lucky stood. "Are you threatening me?"

His laugh surprised her, stroking her senses like warm brandy. "Which of those statements do you find threatening?" he countered silkily.

Lucky glared at him across the expanse of her desk. "You don't scare me one bit, Sam Donahue. Believe me, I've handled men like you before."

"Have you?" Sam's brow rose. "In that case, I shall be looking forward to the experience." He turned to leave, then paused in the doorway. "See you in the trenches, Lucky."

Unwilling to concede the last word, Lucky fired a parting shot of her own. "And I'll see you on the air!"

Then he was gone and she slumped back in her chair. Who'd ever have thought he'd take things so hard? she wondered. All she'd meant to do was beef up business a bit, not start World War III!

So much for good fences making good neighbors.

# 2

LUCKY HAD A HARD TIME keeping her mind on business during the next few days and, as she told herself more than once, it didn't take a genius to figure out that Sam Donahue was the reason why. Though she'd neither seen nor heard from him, tension seemed to crackle in the air between their two lots, its presence every bit as palpable as the strand of electrical wire that marked their common boundary.

If there was one thing Lucky hated, it was waiting for the other shoe to drop. By her own estimation, she'd emerged from their scene in her office a winner. But she didn't delude herself into thinking that Sam was the kind of man who was going to accept defeat and bow out gracefully. No, he would retaliate all right. The only question was how.

It was that very uncertainty that accounted for the fluttery feeling in the pit of her stomach whenever Sam's image floated into her thoughts. It had to be, Lucky told herself as she sat in her office Tuesday morning. There was simply no other explanation. Now that they'd finally had the opportunity to say more than a few words to each other, she'd realized it was just as well that they'd never managed to get together sooner.

From what she'd seen of Sam Donahue, he was arrogant and overbearing—definitely not the sort of man one would keep around for the pleasure of his company. In a way, it was a shame he was so attractive, Lucky thought with a sigh. All those good looks going to waste....

"Are you Lucky?"

Startled, she glanced up and found a teenage girl dressed in spandex pants and a body-hugging tube top, standing in the doorway. "That's me." Lucky rose quickly to her feet. Automatically her hands reached down, smoothing away the creases from the front of her linen skirt. "What can I do for you?"

"My name's Heather Jacobson. I want to buy a car."

Lucky grinned as she walked out from behind her desk. "Then you've come to the right place."

"I hope so. My boyfriend told me your prices are the best."

"He's right." Lucky stepped out onto the asphalt lot then paused, considering which way to head first. She looked back and counted four holes in one of Heather's ears and six in the other. A collection of jangling earrings brushed the girl's shoulders. Definitely not sedan material, Lucky decided. "Who's your boyfriend?" she asked.

Heather blushed. "Ronnie Russo."

"Rockin' Ron?"

"You know him?"

"Sure," said Lucky. "I sold him his first car. It was a bright red Toyota. He came and picked it up on his sixteenth birthday. Didn't have his license yet so he had to have his brother drive it home."

"Yeah," Heather agreed. "He told me about that. He said you drive a tough deal, but you're honest. That's why I came."

Lucky smiled, feeling real pleasure. In her business, that was about the highest accolade one could hope for. "Great," she said, "Why don't we take a walk around and see what catches your eye?"

Ten minutes later, they'd dispensed with such necessary topics as price range and parental permission and had come to a halt beside a low-slung convertible Fiat. Considering its age, the sports car was in very good condition, and Lucky was confident that it would serve its new owner well.

"Now that," said Heather, "is my kind of car."

Lucky frowned thoughtfully. She had a sixth sense for knowing when someone was seriously interested. Despite Heather's emphatic words, the feeling was missing. "I hear a 'but' coming."

It arrived with a loud sigh. "The problem is that my father wants me to buy something big and strong and square. The word he used was uncrushable."

"I see." Lucky nodded, considering. There had to be a way to reconcile the desires of the daughter with the needs of a worried parent. She cast a glance around the lot, then smiled as her gaze lit on the perfect compromise. "Come on," she said, taking Heather's arm. "I've got something to show you."

"Sure," Heather said distractedly. Her fingers trailed along the polished fender of the Fiat as Lucky pulled her away. "Where are we going?"

"Right here." Lucky stopped beside the fence. She waved a hand proudly over a mid-sized car in burnt orange whose looks belied its good breeding. "What do you think?"

Heather eyed the new choice dubiously. "What is it?"

"A 1973 BMW 2002."

"*That's* a BMW?"

Lucky nodded.

"But it looks like a box!"

"That's what the Germans were building in those days."

"And it's orange!"

Lucky swallowed a chuckle. "Big color in the early seventies."

"How many miles does it get to the gallon?"

Lucky nodded with satisfaction. Now they were getting somewhere. "Twenty-five," she said brightly, walking around to open the driver's door. "Why don't you get in and see how it feels? I'll just open up the sun roof for you . . ."

As Lucky kneeled on the front seat of the hot, sun-baked car and reached up awkwardly to crank open the roof, she felt the unmistakable tug of someone's gaze upon her. A glance through the rear window confirmed her suspicions. Across the lot next door, Sam Donahue was standing in front of his showroom. Though several rows of cars separated them, there was no mistaking the direction of his gaze.

Lucky's first thought was that he looked terrific. *What do you care?* asked a small inner voice. Frowning, she shrugged it off.

As usual, Sam was wearing a suit. Lucky recognized its Italian origins immediately. The contoured styling emphasized the breadth of his shoulders and the trim line of his hips. Its color was dove gray. The same, she remembered unwillingly, as Sam's eyes.

She turned and straightened, and Sam's gaze rose with her. Was it her imagination, Lucky wondered, or had the temperature just jumped by ten degrees?

"Here," she said hurriedly, holding open the BMW's door for Heather. "What don't you climb in and see what you think?"

"Great!" said Heather. She slid behind the steering wheel and fit her feet to the pedals. "Hey, this is really terrific! Wait till I tell my Dad!"

What was Sam doing? Lucky wondered distractedly. Though he was no longer in her line of vision, the prickly sensation in the back of her neck assured her of his continuing presence. Surely he must have better things to do than stand around watching her.

"When can I take it for a test drive?"

"What . . . ?" With effort, Lucky reined in her scattered thoughts. "A test drive?"

"You know—once around the block?"

Lucky hated to disappoint the girl, but she had a firm rule about teenagers and test drives. No cars left the lot unless parents were on hand. "Maybe you could bring your father in this weekend," she suggested, "and we'll take the car out then."

"Okay," said Heather, sounding resigned. "Sure."

Lucky knew the moment the teenage girl noticed Sam. One minute she was mooning over the second-hand sports car; the next, her head had lifted and the BMW was all but forgotten. Though the object of her attention had changed, Lucky noted, Heather's rapt expression had not.

"Wow," she breathed softly. "Who's that?"

"Sam Donahue." For some reason, the words came out sounding a great deal more curt than Lucky'd intended. "He owns the dealership next door."

"Maybe I should go over and take a look at what he has to offer."

"Maybe you should." Abruptly Lucky frowned, surprised by the unexpected shaft of irritation that pierced through her. It wasn't as though her lot and Sam's could possibly be in competition, after all. Let Heather shop around. Once the teenager got a look at the prices of Sam's cars, Lucky had no doubt that she would be back.

Her eyes narrowed as she watched Heather thrust out her hips and sashay across the parking lot toward her car. Had she ever been that sure of herself? Lucky wondered. She remembered her teens as a terrible, awkward, in-between stage—too old for girlhood, too young to really be a woman. Thank goodness that was all behind her now.

All at once Lucky's bad mood lifted as her thoughts shifted back to the present. Sam had spied on her. Now it

would be her turn to do the same. It might be interesting to
see how he would handle a teenage girl with an over-
abundant libido and an under-abundance of ready cash.
She cast a glance toward Donahue Motors, then threw back
her head and laughed. This was going to be fun.

IT WAS THE LAUGH that did it, Sam thought. If she hadn't
laughed, hadn't tossed back those golden curls and lifted her
face to the sun in sheer enjoyment of the moment, he might
have been able to turn away and walk back inside to his office. But she had, and he hadn't. Now the question was,
what was he going to do next?

Sam glanced up into the hot noonday sun and frowned.
He'd been standing under its harsh glare for the last ten
minutes, and if there was one thing he hated, it was standing still. Yet for some reason, he'd been perfectly content
doing just that as he watched Lucky Vanderholden pursue
a sale.

He couldn't care less how many of those second-hand
monstrosities she moved. Nor was he apt to learn anything
new about salesmanship by watching her technique. Yet
watching her was exactly what he'd been doing. And enjoying himself, too.

With a quick shrug, Sam pulled off his jacket and slung
it over the railing. Then he unbuttoned his shirtsleeves and
rolled them back to expose strong, muscled forearms covered with a light dusting of dark hair. He didn't know how
Lucky did it. Though the blazing sun baked both their lots
with equal intensity, she looked as cool as a tall yellow daf-
fodil freshened by a summer breeze. Standing straight and
slim beside that ridiculous-looking orange car, she had the
composure and serenity of a queen.

A slow smile lifted the corners of Sam's mouth as he wondered just what it would take to ruffle Lucky Vanderholden's feathers.

Then she turned and their gazes caught. Sam straightened imperceptibly. Instinct sucked in the already tight muscles of his gut. Though he'd never been one to believe in fate, there seemed to be a kind of inevitability to the long moment during which their eyes held.

She stirred something within him, Sam realized, something which had perhaps lain dormant for too long. He hadn't felt so alive, so invigorated in weeks as he had during their brief meeting in her office. She'd involved him fully. His intellect and his senses were equally aroused by the challenge she posed.

If he were honest with himself, he'd admit he'd enjoyed their little contretemps. Just as much as he'd enjoyed the time he'd spent since figuring out the best way to retaliate. Unwittingly, Lucky had renewed the sense of purpose in his life.

Abruptly Sam swung around as a small car careened through the gate and onto his lot. His brow knit when he realized the driver was Lucky's customer, the teenager with the sprayed-on clothing and wild hair. With a jaunty toot of her horn, the girl let the car roll to a stop beside the showroom. Before she'd even had a chance to climb out, a salesman appeared to offer assistance. The girl sent a fleeting look in Sam's direction, then allowed herself to be escorted inside. Immediately Sam put her out of his mind.

When he turned back to Lucky, however, she was gone. It took a moment for him to find her again, tucked into the front seat of the boxy orange car and struggling to close its balky sun roof. On impulse, he started forward. She'd chided him once for his lack of neighborly spirit. There was no time like the present to make up for the omission.

As he reached the fence that marked their common boundary, she was pushing the small handle back up into its niche. For a moment it stuck again, and Sam bit back a smile as he watched Lucky curl her small hand into a fist and ram it home.

"Nowadays we do that with buttons," he said amiably, leaning against the chain link that separated them.

Startled by the sound of his voice, Lucky looked up. She'd just assumed that Sam would follow Heather back into his cool showroom. Or maybe the truth was, she'd hoped he would. Because if he had, then she wouldn't have to deal with him. Instead there he stood, no more than a few feet away, with the sun striking burnished highlights in his brown hair and casting a warm, golden glow to his tan. He looked cocky and confident and incredibly handsome—in short, everything a potential enemy had no right to be. *He's presumptuous*, Lucky reminded herself firmly as she slid out from behind the seat. *And domineering.*

And as long as he didn't smile, she'd probably be okay.

"What do you do with buttons?" she asked, shutting the door to the BMW behind her.

"Open and close sun roofs. In the newer models, they're operated by buttons."

"Those Germans." Lucky shook her head in mock admiration. "You never know what they'll come up with next."

"Don't knock progress, it makes life a lot easier."

"Sure it does. It's just that sometimes it comes with too high a price tag."

"Oh, I don't know," Sam returned easily. He threaded the fingers of his right hand through the fence, and Lucky found herself watching as they curled around the chain link. His fingers were long and slender, the nails clean and well shaped. "I'd say that depends on your point of view."

"Perhaps," Lucky replied, her voice carefully neutral. Looking down, she busied herself with wiping a non-existent speck off the hood of the shiny BMW.

*What's wrong with this picture?* she asked herself. The answer came quickly—everything. In all the time she and Sam had been neighbors, he'd never felt inclined to stop by the fence and chat before. Why now? What was he up to? And why was he in such a good mood? It was almost as though he was enjoying a private joke at her expense.

At that, Lucky straightened, frowning. For pete's sake, now she was beginning to sound paranoid. There was definitely something about Sam Donahue that tended to bring out the worst in her. What harm could there possibly be in his trying to be friendly? Maybe he'd realized that the commercials were never meant as a personal strike against his business. Maybe he'd even forgotten all about them.

Sure, thought Lucky. And maybe she sold cars with a money-back guarantee.

"So," asked Sam. "How's business?"

"Picking up," Lucky said carefully. As far as she was concerned, the topic had all the potential of a mine field. "Yours?"

"I can't complain."

"No." Lucky let her eye roam across the gleaming, well-kept lot. "I don't imagine you would."

Sam followed the line of her gaze and his expression hardened. "Nobody handed me this business, Lucky. I've worked hard for everything I have."

"I never said you hadn't."

Sam wondered how she managed to sound so reasonable and yet give the distinct impression that her true feelings were the exact opposite of what she'd said. She was provoking him deliberately, just as she had the last time they'd met. Then he'd allowed himself to lose his temper. Now, Sam had no intention of making the same mistake again.

"You're very quick at handing out your opinion."

Lucky shrugged. "I have eight brothers and sisters. In my family, if you aren't quick, you get trampled."

*"Eight?"* He hadn't meant to sound so shocked. He cleared his throat and tried again. "There are eight children in your family?"

"Well, nine, actually, if you count me."

"I see," said Sam. Perhaps that explained a few things. "I guess that's why you made those commercials."

"What are you talking about?"

"Just that with a family that size I can see why you might have a need to draw attention to yourself."

Lucky's jaw fell open. Quickly she pulled it shut. "Thank you, Dr. Sigmund Fraud. With psychoanalytical talent like that I can't imagine what you're doing selling cars."

"Come on," Sam said calmly. "You have to admit there can't be very many women who own their own used-car lots, not to mention making television appearances."

Of all the pompous, patronizing men she'd ever met, thought Lucky, Sam Donahue had to take the prize. "I'll have you know there is absolutely nothing wrong with a woman owning and promoting her own business—"

"Nooo..." said Sam, drawing the word out. "It's just your methods that leave something to be desired."

"Methods that happen to be working," Lucky shot back. She had no intention of telling him just how badly she'd needed them to. "That's all that matters."

Out of the corner of her eye, Lucky saw Heather stomp out of Sam's showroom in a huff. Obviously she'd just learned a few truths about the price of life in the fast lane.

With a small glimmer of satisfaction, Lucky watched the teenager climb into her car. Though Heather gunned the motor loudly to announce her departure, Sam never even noticed.

"Then what you're saying," he asked, "is that the end justifies the means?"

That brought her up short. "Sometimes," Lucky said slowly, and watched Sam smile.

"Remember those words," he said softly.

"Don't worry," said Lucky, with more bravado than she felt. "I will." She spun on her heel and walked away.

Sam stood at the fence, enjoying the view, until Lucky reached her office and walked inside. It was clear from the jaunty swing in her stride that she thought she'd bested him. He'd let her believe that a little while longer. After all, she'd find out soon enough that he had a few tricks of his own to unveil.

IN LUCKY'S MIND the most significant thing about the rest of the week was the silence from Donahue Motors. As far as she could see, Sam had all but vanished. Mr. Invisible, she dubbed him, sending quizzical glances toward the high fence that separated them. Though she would have liked to believe that his continuing absence meant she had him on the run, Lucky was much too practical for that. No, Sam was bound to surface and make trouble again, and until that time, there was nothing she could do but wait.

When her sister, Marete, extended an invitation to join her family for dinner over the weekend, Lucky accepted with delight. It had been several weeks since she'd been to her oldest sister's house—a very long time by Vanderholden standards.

Though the siblings ranged in age from nineteen to thirty-six, Lucky's family had remained close both geographically and emotionally. They offered one another advice, support, and most of all, friendship. Lucky was painfully aware that since she was the oldest unmarried child her brothers and sisters had taken up her cause with a fervor. She viewed their attempts at matchmaking as a necessary evil, one that was far outweighed by the numerous benefits her large family provided.

When she arrived at Marete and Bob's Saturday night, her sister wasted no time in getting down to business. She hustled Lucky through the family room, where Bob and their two daughters were watching TV, and into the kitchen where preparations for dinner were in full swing. "So," she began casually, "how's your love life?"

"Dead in the water." Lucky sat down at the counter that separated the two rooms, accepted a paring knife and a cucumber and went to work. "How's yours?"

Marete slanted her a long look down her nose. "We've been married for twelve years. How do you think?"

Lucky glanced toward the family room where Bob was sitting in the middle of the couch, a daughter tucked under each arm. In college he'd been considered a radical. He'd sewn peace signs on his jeans and tied back his long hair with a thong. Now his jeans bore a crease and his hairline had receded past the point of no return. And after all this time, he and Marete were still madly, blissfully in love.

"I'd imagine you're doing fine," said Lucky, careful not to let her envy show. She gave the sliced cucumber an off-hand toss into the salad bowl and went after a tomato.

"We are." Marete grinned. "Marriage is great. You ought to try it."

"That's what I like about you, Marete. Of all my brothers and sisters, you're the most subtle."

"And of all mine, you're the most stubborn."

"Stubborn?" Lucky's brow rose. "Can I help it if I'm not married? Is it my fault if the demand for eligible men far exceeds the supply? Just what exactly would you suggest I do—post a sign in my window that says Available. Inquire Within?"

"Of course not." Marete dug a bag of carrots out of the crisper and slid them across the counter. "But you might try being a little more open to new experiences. How do you expect to meet Mr. Right if you never date?"

Lucky made a disgusted face. "It's not as easy as all that, and you know it. I did a lot of dating when I was younger, and where did it get me? I met tons of men and there wasn't a Mr. Right in the bunch. I met Mr. Party Animal, Mr. On The Rebound, Mr. Workaholic . . ."

Marete rolled her eyes. Pointedly Lucky ignored her.

"Wherever this mythical Mr. Right is hiding, I couldn't smoke him out, and believe me, I tried. Besides, with the way business is going, I just don't have that kind of time to waste anymore."

"But that's exactly my point, it's hardly a waste of time . . ."

Nodding with a token display of interest, Lucky tuned her sister out. She'd heard the sermon so often that by now she could quote chapter and verse. Not that there was any point in trying to stop Marete once she got on a roll. As the oldest girl, she'd taken her duties as their mother's second in command very seriously and that included such things as stating her opinion loudly. Forcibly. Unrequested.

The game show on the TV broke for a commercial and Lucky's gaze flickered in that direction. Although most of her spots ran during the day, Ed Wharton had been pressuring her lately to go all out and try some of the high-priced prime-time slots. Now she was interested to see that the upcoming commercial was indeed for a car dealership, one that suddenly began to look very familiar. . . .

"Wait!" cried Lucky. She leaped up and ran around the counter. "Turn that up!"

Lucky's brown eyes widened as the clear image of Sam's smiling face filled the screen. Damn, but he was photogenic. The camera loved his wide jaw and strong features—and that smile! Lucky felt her stomach drop. Sam's gaze shifted, picked up by another camera, and for a brief, heart-stopping moment, Lucky was sure he was looking directly at her.

Then reality intervened, and she realized with some irritation that that was precisely the effect he was supposed to have. Doubtless every other woman in eastern Pennsylvania had felt it, too.

"What is it?" asked Marete, following her in from the kitchen. "Did Vanna's dress fall off?"

"No such luck," Bob said sadly. "It's only a commercial."

Marete leaned in for a closer look. "Wow, what a hunk. Whatever he's selling, I'm in the market."

"Shh!" cried Lucky. She reached for the volume and turned it up. The commercial was almost over, and what she'd seen thus far had been anything but a pleasant surprise. Sam had copied the tone and style of her own ads with more than a little dexterity. Unconsciously she drew in a breath and held it, waiting for the close.

When it came, it was even worse than she'd feared. The camera drew back to reveal her lot. The cars had been filmed in an evening light that was less than flattering, and after the previous shots of Donahue Motors' shiny new stock, hers couldn't help but look a bit shabby by comparison.

Lucky's hands balled into fists of frustrated rage as she listened to the voice-over say, "Lots of things will get you from here to there. But why settle for merely owning a car, when you can make driving a truly memorable experience instead? Donahue Motors, when only the best will do."

"Wasn't that . . . ?" Bob began. He was looking at Lucky and frowning vaguely.

"It most certainly was!" Lucky huffed.

"Was what?" asked Marete, still trying to figure out what all the fuss was about.

"My lot!" cried Lucky, gesturing dramatically. "My cars! My everything!"

Marete looked at her with fresh appreciation. "Him, too?"

"Him who?" Lucky asked absently, her thoughts still centered on the debacle she'd just seen.

"You know." Marete waved toward the TV where a colored wheel was now spinning while contestants cheered wildly. "Tall, dark and handsome."

"Tall, dark and troublesome is more like it," Lucky muttered irritably. It was an effort not to glare at the TV even though the commercial was obviously long gone.

She just couldn't believe Sam would stoop that low. He might not have liked what she'd said about his cars, but she'd certainly never insulted their quality. All she'd done was refer to their outrageous price tags and let people draw their own conclusions.

Sam's commercial, however, had gone a good deal further than that. Only a moron could have missed the implication that just because Lucky's cars were secondhand their quality was less than the best. And at the prices cars—even used cars—went for these days, who would want to buy something whose value was suspect?

"Troublesome?" Marete grinned in sly delight. "I want to hear all about him."

"No, you don't." Lucky said quickly. She turned to Bob in mute appeal.

"Don't look at me," he said, holding out his hands. "If she listened to a word I said, do you think we'd have orange wall-to-wall carpeting?"

In spite of herself, Lucky had to smile. "When she was little," she confided, "we used to call her Sherman."

"As in General?" asked Bob.

"As in tank."

"All right," said Marete, affecting a wounded tone. "I can take a hint."

"Since when?" Lucky muttered and Bob began to chuckle.

Marete managed to catch both of them in the same glare. "Just tell me one thing. Is that man *really* your new neighbor?"

"Umm-hmm."

"Good." Marete nodded, talking to herself as she walked back into the kitchen. "After dinner, you can help me bake a cake—you know, sort of a welcoming gesture . . ."

"Mar, you don't understand. His dealership has been there nearly seven months."

"Never mind." Marete brushed the objection aside. "Better late than never."

Shaking her head helplessly, Lucky followed along in her sister's wake. So much for any hopes she'd entertained for a nice quiet evening with the family. If she knew Marete, her sister wouldn't rest until they were both up to their elbows in batter.

Sam Donahue, Lucky thought darkly, I'll get you for this!

# 3

PROMPTLY AT NINE the next morning, Lucky drove through the gates of Donahue Motors. She parked her little blue Honda in front of the showroom and sat for a moment collecting her thoughts. She'd never ventured onto Sam's lot before—indeed, there'd been no reason to—and close-up it was even more impressive than she'd imagined.

The low steel and glass building gleamed a soft shade of gray in the morning light, its sleek modern lines providing the perfect showcase for the expensive machines within. Positioned squarely in the front window, a cream-colored Rolls Royce held the place of honor. Just behind and to its left, sat a shiny Mercedes Benz turbo diesel. On the right, a bright red BMW sedan formed the third point in the triangle.

Lucky saw only one desk, but there were several groupings of plush leather chairs designed to afford customers the highest level of comfort. A large TV screen dominated one corner of the room. A VCR and an impressive collection of tapes rested on the table beside it. Spare-no-expense salesmanship, Lucky thought with a sniff. Her customers would rather get out and drive the car themselves than sit down and watch a movie on high-tech performance.

As she climbed from the Honda, her eye scanned the rows of new foreign cars that fanned out in several directions. Their tires were black and thick with tread, their seats and steering wheels covered with protective sheeting. Stickers detailing their myriad array of luxurious options fluttered in the rear windows.

"Conspicuous consumption," Lucky muttered under her breath. Anger, which had shimmered just beneath the surface ever since the night before, now returned full force. As if her puny darts and slings could ever have made the slightest dent in Donahue Motors' armor! But if Sam wanted a fight, then that was exactly what he was going to get. Reaching into the Honda, Lucky swept a large, round parcel up from the passenger seat. Then she straightened, squared her shoulders, and marched inside.

"Can I help you?"

The man who asked the question was young, tan and very eager to please. Lucky looked him coolly up and down. "Where can I find Sam Donahue?"

"I think he's in his office." He glanced toward a hallway at the back of the room. "If you like, I'll go check, Miss...?"

"Never mind." Lucky headed in that direction. "I'll announce myself."

The first four doors in the hallway were open, revealing two offices, a conference room and a bathroom. The one at the end was shut. Lucky rapped once, hard, on the solid wood then opened the door and let herself in.

Sam Donahue was sitting behind a desk on the other side of the room. His head was bent, his attention centered on a sheaf of papers that littered the top of his desk. He'd removed his jacket and tossed it over the arm of a couch that ran along one wall; the knot of his tie was loosened, the top button of his shirt undone. Clearly he had not been expecting visitors.

As Lucky marched into the room, he glanced up briefly, then quickly looked again. The fingers that had been drumming lightly on the edge of the blotter stilled. Surprise came and went in his gray eyes, and Lucky knew she wasn't meant to have noticed. Her earlier impression had been right—Sam wasn't the kind of man who would give up an advantage, any advantage, easily. He started to smile, started to rise, and she quickly moved to forestall both.

"Here," Lucky said, plopping her package down in the middle of his desk. "This is for you."

Sam looked downward quizzically. She'd presented him with a plate whose contents were carefully covered with waxed paper. "What is it?"

"A cake. Welcome to the neighborhood."

He almost laughed and would have, if he hadn't realized just how big a mistake it would be. Instead he cleared his throat. "Thank you . . . I think."

"You're welcome," Lucky snapped. Though she didn't add "I hope you choke on it," the sentiment hovered in the air between them.

Well, thought Sam, studying his gift, this was certainly a novel approach. When she'd first appeared in the doorway, he'd assumed she must have seen the commercial. But now . . . To his chagrin, Sam realized that, for the first time in his life, he didn't know what to think.

"I was at my sister's house last night." Lucky folded her arms across her chest and glared downward pointedly. "Imagine our surprise when we saw you on TV."

This, Sam decided, had to be one of those moments where silence was golden. He unwrapped the edge of the waxed paper, lifted it up, and peered inside. A solid wall of thick, rich, fudge icing met his gaze.

"The next thing I knew I was baking a cake!" Lucky's voice rose, her irritation fanned by the memory. "Baking a cake!" she repeated, sounding every bit as incredulous as Sam was beginning to feel. "And it was all your fault."

Sam let the waxed paper fall back into place. He sat back in his chair, his elbows resting on its arms, his fingers braced in a steeple. "Let me get this straight. Last night you saw one of my commercials on TV, and for some reason, it made you feel like baking?"

"No," Lucky corrected. "Actually it made my sister feel like baking. She took one look at you and decided nothing but a cake would do. Indeed, once she'd seen your smiling face, she hardly talked of anything else all evening."

"I'm flattered." Sam gave up on trying to understand and settled for being entertained instead.

"Don't be. Marete sees you as a potential addition to the Vanderholden family."

"Addition?"

"My sister," Lucky said dryly, "is trying to marry me off."

The steeple collapsed in a tangle of fingers. "To me?"

Lucky walked around the back of the desk, her fingertips trailing along the low credenza, which held a state-of-the-art computer. "You'll do."

Sam found his gaze following her hand as it traced a path idly along the wooden edge. The touch of her fingers was light, almost sensuous, more a caress than an exploration. It didn't take much to imagine what those same fingers would feel like skating lightly over his skin.

She was trying to distract him. Not only that, but she was succeeding.

"I see what you mean about your sister's interest being a double-edged sword," he said carefully. "How about the other seven siblings? How do they feel?"

Lucky glanced up, surprised. She hadn't expected him to remember, had told herself firmly that the bottom line was all that mattered to him. He had no business recalling the size of her family, and she had no business feeling pleased that he had.

Frowning, Lucky stepped back around the desk. She liked the feel of its solid bulk between them. "Marete hasn't had time to consult everyone else yet. After all, we only saw the commercial last night."

Ah yes, the commercial. He'd known they'd be working their way back to that. Under normal circumstances, he'd have thought it a dangerous subject. Now, considering the alternative, the thought of talking business seemed almost tame.

"What did you think of it?" asked Sam. He wondered if she'd play coy. She didn't.

"I hated it, of course. That was a low trick, Sam."

"No lower than some others I've seen recently."

"It most certainly was!"

"Really? How?"

Lucky leaned down, bracing her hands on the edge of the desk. "You implied that my cars are second-rate."

"And you," Sam said calmly, "implied that mine were overpriced."

His serenity only served to infuriate Lucky further. She straightened with regal dignity. "I didn't have to imply that—it's true!"

"Well?"

"Well what?"

"What I said was equally true. As I recall, the phrase second-rate never passed my lips." Once again, Sam realized, Lucky Vanderholden had managed to push his buttons. And once again, he found himself enjoying it. And her. "In fact, to tell the truth, I'm not quite sure what you're getting so upset about—"

Lucky's eyes widened. "For starters, that commercial was an invasion of my privacy."

Silently, Sam nodded. He wondered if she realized just how effective the slim lines of her narrow skirt showed off the shadowed curve of her derriere . . .

"Not to mention unfair business practice—"

Or the way its new, shorter hem accentuated the length of her lovely, slender legs. Did she wear flats for comfort? he wondered, or to minimize her height...?

"Sam!"

He blinked once and looked up.

"Are you listening to me?"

"Of course."

"Then," Lucky said aggressively, "since it doesn't seem to have made much of an impression the first time, I'll repeat what I just said. If you don't cancel that commercial immediately, I plan to consult my lawyer about a suit."

Sam grasped the arms of his chair and rose slowly. He'd let her have the advantage of superior position long enough, perhaps too long considering the turn the conversation had taken. "I wouldn't," he said calmly.

"I don't recall asking for an opinion."

"That's all right, I never wait to be asked."

Sam strode out from behind the desk and pulled a straight-backed chair away from the wall. "Here" he said, setting it beside his desk. "Sit."

Without thinking, Lucky did. Then she watched in consternation as Sam crossed the room to the door. "But—"

"I'll be right back."

Just like that, Lucky thought, fuming as the door slid shut behind him. Who did he think he was, walking out on her? Did he really expect her to simply sit and wait patiently until he decided to return? Apparently he did. It was obvious the interview was not yet over. So far, they hadn't managed to settle a thing.

Actually Lucky was just as glad to have a moment's respite. Sam's office was by no means small, yet with both of them locked within its confines, things had felt uncomfortably close. It had been an effort to maintain the finely honed edge to her anger and an even bigger effort to keep her mind on business.

*You're old enough to know better,* Lucky rebuked herself sternly. Unfortunately age had nothing to do with the potent wave of attraction that poured through her every time Sam was near. She couldn't control it, and that was a problem. If there was one thing she didn't dare do now, it was lose control.

Sighing, Lucky sat back in her seat and wondered where Sam had gone. It was the threat of a lawsuit that had sent him out of the room. That, at least, had managed to get his attention. No doubt he'd gone off in search of ammunition of his own. And whatever it was, she'd better be ready.

Lucky started as the door clicked open behind her. She turned as Sam shouldered it aside and walked into the office, his hands full. She'd expected him to return with papers, or perhaps a cassette. Instead he was carrying a stack of napkins, a knife, and two steaming cups of coffee.

"Will black do?" he asked, sliding back down into his seat.

Automatically Lucky nodded.

Ignoring her incredulous expression, Sam folded back the waxed paper to expose the triple-layer chocolate cake. His hand, holding the knife, hovered in the air above it. "Big or little?"

He had to be kidding.

Sam looked up expectantly. "Well?"

"I don't want any."

"Dieting?" Sam's tone was sympathetic, but his lips curved into a tantalizing half smile.

"No," Lucky said succinctly. "Angry."

"So I see." Sam cut two thick slabs, slipped them onto a pair of napkins and placed one in front of each of them.

"Damn it, Sam, you're not taking me seriously!"

"On the contrary. I take your attitude very seriously. It's your threats I find hard to credit—especially since I tried out and rejected essentially the same ideas myself two weeks ago. Of course, you can mount a lawsuit if you like, but you haven't a prayer of winning and we both know it."

He was right, of course. Lucky had watched Sam's commercial with a discerning eye, and it had come as no surprise that he'd been every bit as careful filming her lot as she'd been filming his. She'd only thrown out the idea because she was angry. And Sam, damn him, hadn't wasted any time in throwing it right back in her face.

Sam waited for Lucky to begin eating. When a moment passed, and she continued to ignore the cake between them, he merely shrugged and dug in himself. He lifted a forkful to his lips, then paused as a sudden thought struck him.

Lucky caught the brief moment of hesitation and smiled. "You're wondering just how low I'd stoop, aren't you?"

"The thought had crossed my mind."

"Don't worry, it's not booby-trapped. The worst that that cake can offer you is a sugar high and impending tooth decay."

Sam trusted her, though he didn't know why. If past experience was anything to go by, she was dying to make trouble for him. Slowly he slid the fork between his lips and trapped the morsel on his tongue. The devil's food cake was moist and rich, the icing dark and sweet.

To his surprise, the bite went down with something akin to relief. He hadn't wanted her to disappoint him, Sam realized. The thought did not comfort him in the least. Disconcerted, he fell back on social convention. "Wonderful," he said, sectioning off another piece. "I must send my compliments to the chef."

"Consider them sent," said Lucky. She wistfully eyed the untouched slice of cake on her side of the desk before gathering her purse and standing up.

"You?" Sam shot her a startled look.

Lucky drew her lips into a thin line. If she hadn't, she might have smiled. "Marete can burn Pop-Tarts. Somebody has to rescue her from herself."

"You're a woman of many surprises, Lucky."

She'd started across the room and now, as she reached the door, Lucky stopped. "That line is so old, it has whiskers."

Sam's brow lifted. "Funny you should think I'd want to hand you a line."

Was it? Lucky wondered. Unless her imagination was working overtime, she wasn't the only one feeling the subtle undercurrent that eddied relentlessly between them.

"Actually," she said, "I don't see anything funny about our relationship at all."

It was then that Sam grinned, a slow, lazy smile that spread across his face and fanned a spray of tiny lines out from the corners of his eyes. Lucky's fingers tightened involuntarily on the doorknob, as she felt a sudden, unexpected rush of heat. All at once, the pounding of her heart seemed very loud.

With a feeling akin to desperation, she pulled open the door and started down the hallway. She was moving quickly, but not fast enough to escape Sam's parting words.

"That," he said with satisfaction, "is what makes it so intriguing."

LUCKY SAT AT HER DESK and unwrapped the turkey sandwich she'd brought for lunch. Her morning had been incredibly busy, but she still hadn't managed to put the gleaming image of Donahue Motors out of her mind. On her way out of Sam's office, she hadn't been able to resist stopping to peek at a few of the price stickers that adorned the shiny automobiles in his showroom, and the numbers she'd seen listed there so casually had made her gasp. She'd known Rolls Royces didn't come cheap, but the very thought of paying six figures for a car—even one that was beautifully hand-crafted—was simply ridiculous!

Clearly, Lucky decided, the people who needed that sort of status symbol had never learned to appreciate the finer things. Growing up as she had in a house filled with children, hand-me-downs had been a simple fact of life. Almost everything she'd had, from clothes, to books, to toys, was used. But that, Lucky had come to realize, didn't diminish their value in any way.

Rather than feeling as though she'd been given second best, Lucky had learned at an early age to appreciate the items as much for their heritage as for their present utility. Instead of longing for something new, she'd delighted in jeans that were already faded and school books with helpful notes scribbled in the margins. She'd seen, too, the love and care that went into preserving each child's belongings for the next: the soft baby blankets so carefully wrapped in tissue until they would be needed yet again; the nights her mother sat up late, taking in one sister's prom dress so that another might wear it to homecoming.

Those were the things that really mattered. Lucky knew that was what grounded you and gave you a sense of who you really were. And all those shiny new trinkets that seemed so important one year and so out of date the next were nothing more than insubstantial baubles whose only worth could be measured in dollars and cents. There was nothing wrong with a car with a past. Lucky believed history added a warmth and richness to the present that couldn't be found at any price.

When the phone rang, she reached up absently, plucking off her earring as she fitted the receiver to her ear.

"Lucky? It's Sam."

He hadn't needed to identify himself. She'd recognized the wonderful, deep cadence of his voice immediately. Lucky straightened in her chair as her dreamy, introspective mood faded. "Yes?" she asked warily.

"I'm calling about your visit this morning. We never really managed to get anything settled—"

"That was hardly my fault!" Lucky cut in. A moment passed, then she heard Sam sigh. There was a quiet sort of resignation to the sound, almost as though he couldn't figure out why she insisted on making things between them so difficult. All at once, Lucky found herself wondering the same thing.

"Look, I didn't call to assign blame," he began slowly. "I was just thinking that maybe if we try again, we might do a little better."

"Try again?" Lucky echoed. They could talk until the cows came home, but that didn't mean that the two of them were ever going to agree.

"I'd like to pay you back for the cake. Have dinner with me tonight, Lucky, and we'll talk—really talk. No sparring, no fighting—just two neighbors trying to resolve a little dispute in a friendly way."

Though it crossed her mind that she ought to refuse, she never, even for a moment, considered doing so. There were too many issues still unresolved between them. And, Lucky mused, considering the amount of time she'd spent thinking about him lately, business might turn out to be the least of them. . . .

"Lucky?"

"Sorry, just thinking."

"If tonight's bad—"

"No, tonight's fine. I'd like very much to have dinner with you, Sam."

"Good." Sam took her address and they chose a time. As Lucky hung up the phone she realized she was already figuring out what to wear. It was just going to be a friendly dinner, she reminded herself firmly. Sam was only making a neighborly gesture in giving them a much-needed opportunity to sit down calmly and try to patch up their differences.

Sure, said a tiny inner voice, that's exactly what the Trojans thought when they accepted that big wooden horse.

# 4

LUCKY HAD INTENDED to close up at five, leaving herself with plenty of time to get home and prepare for her date with Sam. But an unexpected surge of business caught her by surprise, and as things turned out, it was after six before the last customer had been satisfied and the office locked for the night. By the time she had battled rush-hour traffic and pulled the Honda into the driveway alongside of her small Victorian house, she was feeling frazzled and more than a little irritated. It was hardly an auspicious omen for the evening to come.

She dashed up the steps to the front porch and had started to fit her key into the lock, when she realized that the door was already open. Nudged by her fingertips, it swung inward. The loud noise of a cartoon being watched at high volume floated out into the evening air. Huckleberry Hound, unless Lucky missed her guess.

"Hello?" she called, still hesitating on the porch.

"Oh good, you're back!"

The words had scarcely had a chance to register before the boy who had uttered them appeared—a tall, gangly adolescent with a thatch of thick, wheat-colored hair. He bounded out into the hallway and covered the distance to the door in three long strides. Grabbing Lucky up, he swung her around exuberantly.

"Ken!" Lucky finally managed as she landed unsteadily on her feet. "Why aren't you at school? Is something wrong?"

"Nope, everything's just grand."

"Then why...?"

"You know how college dorms are—sometimes you just need to get away for a night. I hope you don't mind, I made myself at home."

"Of course not," Lucky said weakly as she followed him back to the den. A newspaper scattered across the floor and the remains of a cheese steak sandwich, balanced precariously on the couch, attested to the validity of Ken's claim. She crossed the room and turned down the volume on the small TV. "How did you get in?"

"No problem. Mom and Dad always kept their spare key over the ledge in the garage. It was the first place I looked."

"Terrific," Lucky muttered. She wasn't unhappy to see her brother. Family visits, no matter how unexpected, were always a pleasure. It was just that tonight she had other things on her mind.

Oblivious to her concern, Ken flopped back on the couch. He lifted his feet, then set them down with a resounding thunk on top of the coffee table. "So, what's for dinner?"

"Dinner?" Lucky nodded toward the crust-filled plate. "It looks like you just ate."

"I had to have something to tide me over until you got back."

"Of course," Lucky said dryly. Her nineteen-year-old brother's voracious appetite was fast on the way to becoming a family legend. "You'd better hope there's a pizza in the freezer because I'm going out. I've got a date."

"A date?" Ken leaped from the couch, then followed as Lucky started up the stairs. "Who with?"

Lucky cast him a baleful glance over her shoulder. "Nobody you know."

"What's his name?" Ken persisted. They reached Lucky's bedroom, and he lowered his lanky frame down onto her bed.

"Sam," Lucky replied distractedly as she pulled open her closet door and studied her options.

"Sounds awful."

"Oh?" Lucky pulled out a navy linen shirtwaist dress and tossed it onto a chair. "Why?"

"If that isn't a solid, dependable name I don't know what is. I'll bet he's forty and bald."

"Wrong. Try thirty-five and gorgeous."

"Then why on earth are you wearing that?"

Lucky spun around, surprised. "What's the matter with it?"

Ken reached out to finger the navy dress derisively. "If a girl ever dressed like this for a date with me, I'd know I was in trouble."

Lucky shot him a look. "I've seen most of your girl-friends, Ken. Take it from me, you *are* in trouble."

"At least they don't wear clothes that have 'don't touch me' written all over them."

"Perfect," Lucky said firmly. She unzipped her skirt and stepped out of it. "This is a business date."

"Business date?" Ken hooted. "That's an oxymoron if I ever heard one. Why bother to go out with the guy at all, why not just send him a memo?"

Why indeed? Lucky wondered as she stripped down to her slip. The easy answer, of course, was because Sam had asked. But the real reason went much deeper than that. As much as Lucky found him brash and his business tactics irritating, Sam was also the most interesting man she had met in a very long time.

Perhaps their relationship was bound to remain adversarial. Or perhaps they were destined for something more.

Either way, Lucky wasn't about to pass up the chance to find out.

"Here," Ken said and Lucky looked up to find him holding out one of her favorite dresses—a shimmering red silk. "Wear this one."

"You're as bad as Marete," Lucky muttered, snatching the dress from his hand and tossing it on top of her choice.

"Heaven forbid."

"My sentiments exactly." Lucky stared pointedly at the door. "Do you mind? I'd like to take a shower."

"How do you like that? Give the girl her own bathroom and she begins to get uppity. Don't forget," Ken added as he started for the door, "I was the one who watched you put on your first bra upside down."

"You were also the one who tacked it to the bulletin board in the boys' locker room."

"I was famous for a whole month," Ken remembered fondly.

"Out!" cried Lucky. "If you want to make yourself useful, you can go downstairs and straighten up before Sam gets here."

"Sure, take your time. If your date arrives, I'll be happy to keep him occupied for you."

She should have taken that as a warning, Lucky realized twenty minutes later as she hurried down the stairs. When the doorbell had rung, she'd been stepping out of the shower. There'd been nothing to do but take Ken at his word and let him play host for a few minutes while she put on her makeup and slipped on her dress. But now, hearing the laughter that emanated from the front parlor, Lucky wondered if she'd made a mistake. Obviously the two men were enjoying themselves. Unfortunately, Lucky was too well acquainted with her brother's weird sense of humor to imagine that was a good sign.

She got as far as the arched doorway, then paused. Sam and Ken were seated side by side on the couch. A large book was spread open on the table in front of them. With a grimace, Lucky noted that they were looking at her fifth-grade yearbook picture—the one where she wore braces and pigtails.

Then her gaze rose and her eyes met Sam's. His were filled with amusement and something else—pleasure, Lucky realized—and she felt her heart give a little skip. Her cheeks suffused with heat, then the sensation traveled downward until her whole body seemed consumed with it. All at once, Lucky wished she'd followed her first impulse and stayed with the navy linen. The silk was too soft, too clinging, too red. . . .

"You look lovely," Sam said warmly. He rose to his feet, the yearbook forgotten on the table.

"Thank you," Lucky managed. She started toward him, then hesitated. A kiss was certainly inappropriate, yet a handshake seemed wrong, too. She took a deep breath and tried another tack. "Can I get you something to drink?"

"I already offered," Ken broke in. "He isn't thirsty." Lucky slanted her brother a look. He read "get lost" and decided to ignore it. "I was just showing Sam some old pictures."

"So I see." Lucky edged over to the table and swept the yearbook shut. "I'm sure he was thrilled."

"He liked the one of you playing field hockey the best."

Lucky closed her eyes and stifled a groan.

"It showed a different side of you than I've seen thus far," Sam commented, laughter edging his tone. "You look quite fierce when you're carrying a big stick."

"And sometimes," said Lucky, glaring at her brother, "even when I'm not."

"Isn't that a great dress?" Ken chattered on blithely. "I picked it out myself."

in everything from the sun's warm kiss to a wash of crisp night air. Her response was unconscious, almost primitive, her movements no more studied than those of a cat curling up to bask before a warm fire.

Usually Sam was comfortable without conversation. He admired women who felt no need for constant chatter. Now, however, the silence felt incomplete. In the time they'd spent together, he'd found Lucky Vanderholden both infuriating and intriguing. Tonight, he added *tantalizing* to the list. Yet, incredibly, he still knew almost nothing about her.

He'd declared a truce, thought Sam, but that didn't necessarily mean that Lucky would uphold it. No doubt, in her own endearingly bull-headed way, she'd probably ruin his dinner by demanding that they talk shop. And if that happened, they'd be bound to argue.

Clearly, Sam decided, if they were ever going to get past the thrust and parry stage, the time to lay the groundwork was now, when Lucky looked so sweetly at peace with herself and the world.

"I like your brother," he began.

Lucky opened her eyes slowly. "At the moment, that makes one of us."

So much for sweetness, Sam told himself, then grinned. Oh hell, he'd always liked a challenge better, anyway. "He was only looking out for your best interests."

Lucky cocked a brow. "Is that why he pulled out my old Sacred Heart yearbook?"

"Actually," Sam admitted, "that came later."

"Somehow I just know I'm going to live to regret this, but what came earlier?"

"That was when he grilled me about my prospects, my intentions and the state of my health."

Lucky swallowed abruptly and sat up straight. "And what did you tell him?"

"Propitious on all three counts."

"Someday I'm going to murder that boy," Lucky said conversationally as Sam flicked on his signal and turned through the brick gateposts of a new condominium complex. "I probably should have done it years ago."

"You don't look like the type to carry a grudge."

"I'm not," Lucky said with a sigh. "That's probably how Ken's managed to survive this long. We Vanderholdens are incredibly fast to fly off the handle, but then our anger fades just as quickly. We spend half the time at each other's throats, and the other half moaning that we don't get together often enough."

"I should think a family the size of yours would have too hard a time coordinating schedules to see each other very often," Sam commented. The BMW turned into a reserved parking space and rolled to a stop.

"Not at all," Lucky replied as she opened her door. "It's important to us, so we make the time, and the effort. Besides, we've all stayed in the area, so it's not as big a job as you might think."

"What I think, if you don't mind my saying so, is that your gatherings must look something like Macy's parade."

"I guess they do," Lucky admitted, following Sam up the steps. Somehow she'd never thought of things in quite that light before. "What about you—do you see your family often?"

"Hardly ever. My mother and stepfather moved to Arizona five years ago. Mostly we keep in touch by phone." Sam didn't sound perturbed in the least by a state of affairs that would have left Lucky feeling positively bereft. He swung open the door and ushered her inside. "And as for siblings, I haven't any—"

"None?"

Sam shook his head.

"Well, then, I guess that explains it." Lucky looked at Sam and waited, wondering if he'd remember his own similar comment when he'd learned the size of her family. To her satisfaction, she saw recognition dawn.

"Explains what?" he asked cautiously.

"That habit you have of thinking you know everything. It's obvious you weren't bossed around enough as a child."

"Either that," said Sam, waggling his eyebrows wickedly, "or maybe I *do* know everything."

"Fat chance!" Lucky laughed. She wished, not for the first time, that Sam wasn't quite so devastatingly attractive. Clearly, the sense of outrage she'd felt toward him would have been easier to maintain if he had been, as Ken had guessed, forty and balding.

Then again, Lucky realized, she'd been telling the truth when she'd told Sam she'd never been any good at nursing a grievance. Strike back, blow off steam, then let it go—that was her style. It had always stood her in good stead before, there was no reason to doubt that it would do so now.

"I'll grant you one thing." Lucky flashed him a saucy grin. "If the smells coming from your kitchen are any indication, you *do* know how to cook."

"I like to eat. One follows the other," Sam said modestly. He waved toward the sunken living room that opened off the hall. "Go on in and make yourself comfortable. I just want to check in the kitchen and make sure everything's progressing according to plan."

As Sam headed off one way, Lucky went the other. Two steps down left her standing on a plush, deep pile carpet she mentally tagged industrial gray. The walls of the room were painted cream. The couch and loveseat were covered in matching cream leather. They faced each other over a chrome and glass coffee table that held a spherical sculpture, positioned dead center, and nothing more.

A single Breuer chair and another glass table were grouped in one corner, as though placed in solitary confinement. Chrome shelving on the other wall held a television, stereo and various other electronic equipment. Track lighting added a muted glow. The effect was spare, glossy and very high tech. And Lucky was quite sure she'd never seen such a disgustingly impersonal room in her entire life.

Where were the odds and ends? she wondered. The magazines? The knickknacks? For pete's sake, she thought, where were the dirty socks?

Lucky walked over to the couch and debated sitting down. No creases marred the smooth leather surface. No scuff marks spoiled the pale, pristine color. If anybody'd ever used the room before, it certainly bore no signs. Shaking her head, Lucky spun around, quite certain she'd be happier in the kitchen. No matter what it looked like, it couldn't be worse than this.

She'd just reached the steps when Sam turned the corner and hopped down. Too late to check, his momentum carried him into her. Instinctively Sam reached out with both hands and grasped Lucky's shoulders. The same sort of unthinking reaction on her part placed Lucky's hands on his waist.

"Sorry," she said quickly.

"No, it was my fault." Even though it was no longer necessary, Sam found he was loathe to relinquish his hold. The feel of her palms, riding just above the curve of his hips, was light but firm. In his mind, a fantasy surfaced.... Lucky was using the hold to pull their bodies closer together... Then as quickly as it had come, it was gone, and only the tightness in his gut remained.

"I'm okay now," Lucky said softly. She should have stepped back, but somehow, she hadn't. "You can let go."

"So can you," Sam pointed out. His thumbs began to move slowly, tracing the winged arch of her collarbone. "Where were you going?"

"I...um..." Lucky drew a breath and frowned. She wasn't in the habit of forgetting what she was about to say. Then again, she wasn't in the habit of being stroked through silk, of having her skin feel as though it was turning to warm honey beneath a man's touch. "I was on my way to look for you."

Sam's lips curved. "Miss me?"

"Yes..." Lucky began, then changed her mind. "No..."

She looked up into Sam's eyes and saw deep gray pools of smokey desire. Did they reveal his needs, she wondered, or were they merely a reflection of her own? Then her gaze drifted lower and found his mouth. His lips were full, firm and slightly parted. Mesmerized, Lucky found she didn't have the will to drag her gaze away. Seconds passed, and neither one moved. Finally Lucky could stand the suspense no longer.

"Are you going to kiss me, or what?"

Sam looked at her for a long, thoughtful moment. "I don't know," he said finally. "Would you like me to?"

Yes! Lucky's thoughts screamed in silent response. Yes, she wanted him to kiss her. She wanted him to pull her close, to hold her trapped against his solid chest, to cradle her in his arms and kiss her until she couldn't possibly remember why the whole thing was such a bad idea in the first place. What she wanted, for the first time in her liberated life, was for a man to take without asking permission what she knew better than to give.

"No," she said slowly. "I guess not." Lucky shrugged out of his grasp, telling herself that she wasn't disappointed in the least by the ease with which he let her go.

Frowning, Sam let her step away. "You *guess* not?"

Damn, but she was the most irritating person he'd ever met. Usually, he was very adept at interpreting a woman's signals. But with Lucky, he was way out in left field.

"Is this a test?' he demanded.

Lucky looked up, surprised. "Of what?"

"You tell me—you're the one who asked the question."

"Oh for pete's sake!" Lucky snapped. She wasn't even sure herself what it was that she wanted from Sam. And if she couldn't understand her own feelings, she certainly had no intention of trying to explain them to him. "Now I know why we fight all the time."

"Really? Why?" Sam watched the color bloom in her cheeks, the heated rise and fall of her breast, then quickly lifted his hands and shoved them into his pockets. It was either that or slide them around her.

"Because you're an arrogant, contrary sonofa—"

"Careful," Sam warned. To his relief, amusement overtook desire. "Is that the way the nuns taught you to talk?"

Lucky swore softly under her breath. "I knew letting Ken meet you at the door was a mistake."

"Oh, I don't know. I rather enjoyed my trip down memory lane."

His smile tugged away at the last vestiges of Lucky's irritation until she couldn't even remember what it was she'd been so mad about in the first place. "I'll tell you what," she proposed. "You forget that you ever saw that yearbook, and I'll try to overlook the fact that your living room..." Abruptly she stopped, aghast at what she'd almost said.

"What about my living room?" Sam's gaze swept around the space, reassuring himself that it was much the way it had always been.

"Nothing," Lucky said quickly. "Let's go—"

"You don't like it," Sam stated flatly.

"I didn't say that."

"You didn't have to, it's written all over your face."

"It's not that I don't like it, exactly...."

"Then what?"

Lucky took a deep breath and plunged in. "I hate it."

"Well then," said Sam, his voice dangerously reasonable. "That's much better."

"You don't understand. It's just that everything is so...new."

"I see," Sam replied, though he didn't at all. "Would you rather I'd picked up my furniture at the Salvation Army?"

"No, of course not." Lucky paused for another look. "At least, I don't think so."

"How reassuring."

Lucky realized she wasn't getting through to Sam at all. All at once, it seemed very important to make him understand. "The room has no warmth, no feeling. It looks like a display room in a model home, like nobody really lives here."

Sam glanced around in consternation. He'd never noticed whether the room had, or didn't have, warmth. Indeed, he'd never given the issue a moment's thought. The room was simply a convenience, something that was there when he needed it. Certainly it lacked the cheerful, unselfconscious clutter he'd seen in Lucky's house, but in his mind that was hardly grounds for condemnation.

"Where are your pictures?" Lucky continued, aiming a sweeping gesture at the wealth of empty surfaces.

"What pictures?"

"You know, photographs of your parents, or of yourself—hugging the family dog, graduating from college, cooing on a bearskin rug?"

"We weren't a hugging and cooing family. Besides, I have a picture of my parents." To Sam's surprise, he sounded almost defensive.

"One?"

"In the bedroom."

"Well," Lucky allowed. "I guess that's a start."

Sam draped a companionable arm around Lucky's shoulders and shepherded her toward the kitchen. "Think of it this way. At least I don't have to live in fear of having my most embarrassing moments dredged up and paraded before the company."

Lucky smiled at that. He did have a point. "Are you going to feed me now?" she asked, changing the subject.

"Umm-hmm. Hungry?"

"Starved."

"Good." Sam directed her to a breakfast nook at the end of the kitchen where a butcher block table was beautifully set with crystal and bone china. "I like an appreciative audience."

He was certainly going to have that, Lucky realized, her eyes widening at the array of steaming dishes Sam brought to the table. She wouldn't have expected him to be so comfortable in the kitchen. The man who had argued, harassed and infuriated her in the office had hardly seemed the domestic type. Yet obviously she'd been wrong because here, as always, Sam was totally confident, totally in control, all without sacrificing one iota of the virile masculinity that drew her like a magnet.

"Do you like Italian?"

"Love it." Sam lifted the top off one warming dish and Lucky inhaled deeply. "Veal piccata?"

"And fettucini alfredo. I hope you meant it earlier when you said you weren't dieting."

Lucky pulled up short as mention of their earlier meeting brought another thought. "When did you have time to do all this?"

"To tell the truth, there wasn't that much to do." Sam filled a plate with creamy pasta and passed it across the table. "I was planning to cook this dinner for myself so I had all the ingredients. All I had to do was double them."

Lucky's fork stopped in the air, poised midway to her mouth. "Do you mean to say you actually eat like this every night?"

"Mostly." Sam shrugged. "Just because I'm eating alone, I don't see any reason to wolf down a frozen dinner in front of the TV."

Lucky flushed guiltily, thinking of how many tired nights she had done exactly that. "You're going to make some woman a wonderful husband."

"Maybe," Sam said mildly.

"You don't sound too anxious."

"I guess I'm not." Sam turned his attention back to the food. "Or maybe I just haven't met the right woman yet."

It was interesting the way his words mirrored those Lucky had said to her sister. It only confirmed her theory that dating in the eighties was no picnic no matter which side of the trenches you were on. On the other hand, it seemed they'd finally found something on which they could agree.

Lucky should have found that reassuring, but instead her reaction was just the opposite. She was much more comfortable when Sam remained firmly ensconced in the role she'd assigned to him—that of business associate and adversary. If he stepped out of that slot and into other areas of her life, she had a sneaking suspicion all hell was going to break loose.

But only if she let it, Lucky reminded herself firmly. This was a business dinner, after all. They were together to discuss ad campaigns and bottom lines. Certainly there was nothing too risky involved with that.

But somehow, Lucky simply couldn't bring herself to broach the topic of business as she dug, with sybaritic abandon, into the delicious meal Sam had prepared. It seemed wholly inappropriate to start a discussion that was bound to lead to problems while her taste buds were tingling with unaccustomed delight. Instead, she contented herself with eating everything she'd been given, then holding out her plate for a second helping,

Sam should have known serving her pasta was going to be trouble. He watched Lucky dig into the second plateful with the same lusty appreciation she'd shown to the first. But then, before tonight he'd never realized what a sensuous food fettucini could be.

Again and again, Sam's eyes were drawn to the graceful movement of Lucky's hands as she deftly twirled the long noodles, then lifted them to her mouth. The delight with which she slid the fork between her moist pink lips, then slowly withdrew it was enough to make him squirm in his seat. When a drop of the smooth, creamy sauce hovered briefly at the corner of her mouth, he was already reaching for his napkin as the pointed tip of her tongue flicked out to lap it up.

She was driving him crazy and for all the wrong reasons, too. They were supposed to be talking, discussing, resolving their differences. He'd been afraid they might wind up arguing. It had never, even for a moment, crossed his mind that they might wind up in bed. But now Sam admitted to himself that that was exactly where he wanted them to be. Ever since he'd released Lucky from his embrace, he'd wanted nothing more than to hold her once again in his arms.

Of course on a rational level, such an idea was nothing short of madness. And the thought that he, sensible, sane Sam Donahue, should be entertaining it was crazier still.

He'd spent his whole life carefully plotting the alternatives—forming a clear vision of where he wanted to be, then taking the safest possible route to get there. And there would be nothing safe or sensible about leaping precipitously into a relationship with his headstrong, impetuous neighbor. Of that he was quite sure.

It was time to slow down, Sam realized. Time to concentrate on taking things one step at a time.

With effort, he managed to take his own advice. Through the rest of the meal and the clean-up that followed, Sam kept the conversation light and totally impersonal. With Lucky's compliance, they found themselves establishing a very comfortable rapport. Later, when both had agreed on the need for an early night, they made the drive back in companionable silence.

As they pulled into her driveway Lucky saw that nearly every light in the house was on. When Sam took her hand and walked her up the steps to the door, the faint sound of rock music confirmed that her brother was still up. So much for privacy, Lucky thought with a sigh before putting her brother firmly out of her mind.

"You know," she said, turning to Sam, "we never did get around to talking business."

His hand came up to cradle her chin, his fingers warm and strong against the smooth line of her jaw. "Perhaps that's just as well."

Lucky gazed quizzically upward. "Why?"

"Do me a favor," Sam said softly. He'd been a patient man all evening. He'd be damned if it wasn't time for step two. "Just don't ask any questions."

His mouth came down to cover hers, and Lucky's eyes slid shut as she took the step forward that fit her into Sam's arms. The lights, the music, her brother, all were forgotten as she lost herself in the sweetness of Sam's touch. His lips pressed softly until her mouth opened, warm and pliant, beneath his. Her tongue reached out, touching, teasing, then withdrawing as Lucky tipped back her head in invitation.

This was what she'd wanted earlier when Sam had held her in his arms. And now she knew that she'd been right to want, that her desire for Sam was as intense as it was inevitable. Her head whirled, responding giddily to the erotic rhythm of his kiss. With a small moan she gave herself up to sensation, feeling weightless and boneless and hot as molten honey in Sam's embrace.

He pulled her close and then closer still, until their bodies touched from shoulder to thigh. His hands traced the curve of her spine, his fingers gliding gently over the smooth silk. Lucky made a small whimpering noise in the back of her throat, and Sam knew he wanted more. Sanity and common sense were in grave danger of flying out the window. At the moment, he would watch them go without a pang.

No sooner had the treacherous thought crossed his mind, however, than the decision was abruptly taken out of his hands. The porch light flicked on, then just as quickly off again. Immediately Lucky leaped back out of his arms.

Sam swore softly under his breath. "Ken?"

"I'm afraid so."

With that, the front door swung open. "Sorry about that," Ken announced. "I thought I heard a car pull up and figured I'd turn the light on for you. Look, go back to what you were doing, don't let me disturb you—"

"It's all right," Lucky interrupted. With each word her brother spoke, the romantic mood that had enveloped them slipped farther and farther away. "We were just saying good night."

"Go right ahead."

"Thank you," Sam said firmly. He grasped the knob and pulled the door shut so that he and Lucky were alone once more. "Your brother has abominable timing."

"I know."

Sam cocked a brow. "I take it he isn't as anxious as Marete to marry you off?"

"Hardly," Lucky replied, laughing in spite of herself.

"Good," Sam said, almost to himself as he turned away. "If the entire Vanderholden clan ganged up on me, I think I might begin to worry."

"Sam?" Lucky called after him as he started down the steps. "Are you going to take your commercial off the air?"

Sam paused and turned around. "No. Are you?"

Slowly Lucky shook her head.

"I'm glad to hear that."

"You are?"

Sam grinned, that irresistible half smile that did such queer things to her insides. "It would seem a shame for us to come to terms now, especially when we've just found out how enjoyable negotiating can be."

A shame? thought Lucky. It would be a crime. With a shake of her head, she opened the door and went inside.

# 5

"TRUST ME, LUCKY, you've got to fight fire with fire."

It was mid-afternoon Monday, and Lucky and Ed Wharton were out walking around the lot, assessing once again the direction her ad campaign had taken. Lucky paused beside a butterscotch-colored Pinto and looked at the advertising rep pointedly. "It's precisely that attitude that caused the problem in the first place."

"That's exactly my point!" A thick cigar, clutched between Ed's stubby fingers, left a trail of smoke as he waved his hand through the air. "Donahue's a savvy businessman, I'll give him that. At least when he was attacked, he knew enough not to take it lying down."

"I haven't taken anything lying down," Lucky said mildly.

"Oh no?" Ed's chest puffed in surprise. "Well that's what it looks like to me, and to the rest of the world, too, if you don't start answering those commercials of his with some fire power of your own."

"More commercials won't solve the problem, they'll only make it escalate. Besides, other than you, hardly anybody seems to have noticed that it's my lot that's featured in Sam's ad. I hate to admit it, but maybe I overreacted—"

"When it comes to advertising, there's no such thing as overreacting."

"There is when you're spending my money. That much air time doesn't come cheap, you know."

"Of course not." Ed leaned back on the economy car's hood. It sagged visibly beneath his bulk. "If it did, every

Tom, Dick and Louie would be on the airwaves. But you have to admit it, it's been worth it, hasn't it?"

Yes, thought Lucky, she did have to admit that. But not necessarily out loud, and certainly not to Ed Wharton, whose only goal it seemed, was to encourage her to pour her entire life savings into his advertising budget. Still Ed was right. The commercial had accomplished everything she'd hoped for, and more.

Traffic was up and sales with it. Not only that, but a number of her customers had mentioned seeing her on TV as though, in their minds, she'd achieved some sort of instant celebrity status. One little boy had even gone so far as to ask for her autograph!

The only person who hadn't been pleased, of course, was Sam Donahue. Sam, who had asked her to his house to talk business; who had kissed her on her front porch in a way that she'd never been kissed before; and who had then had the nerve to let the last four days to go by without so much as a word.

"Well, Lucky?" Ed prompted. "What are you going to do?"

She shrugged absently, still mired in her own thoughts. "What would you suggest?"

"Prime-time coverage for starters—"

"Too expensive."

"And a splashy new spot," Ed continued on as if she hadn't spoken. His eyes raked up and down over her slender body critically. "You've got to lose the conservative image. Try something a little slinky, a little low cut . . ."

Lucky couldn't hold back a laugh. "I'm selling cars, Ed, not myself."

"Shows how much you know. I'm the expert around here, remember?"

"And I'm the one who pays the bills," Lucky said firmly. "For the time being, we'll stay with what we have."

Ed leaped up. A long ash fell from the tip of his cigar, smearing the front of his shirt. "You'll be sorry. You don't think Donahue's sitting over there biding his time, do you?"

"Quite frankly, I don't know what Sam's doing," Lucky said. A trace of irritation hovered on the edge of her tone. "But I do know what I intend to do and that's stay with the commercial we've already got."

Ed was still muttering under his breath about dire consequences as he heaved his solid frame into his car and drove away. Lucky watched him go, then walked back into her office and sat down at her desk. She'd spent the last four days determined not to think about Sam Donahue, and the last four days thinking about him, anyway. In that regard, Ed's visit hadn't helped one bit.

By now, she'd seen his commercial numerous times. Indeed, more than once she'd caught herself scanning the local stations hoping to find it. She'd only wanted to see how widespread his coverage was, Lucky had told herself defensively as she used the remote control to zap from one channel to another. But that didn't explain why she sat through the ad time after time, her eyes never leaving Sam's face.

Lucky's fingers drummed on the desk top impatiently as she glared at the silent phone. So he liked negotiating with her, did he? Then why didn't he call so they could do it some more?

Perhaps she was being unfair, Lucky mused. There could have been a thousand reasons why Sam hadn't gotten in touch. For one, maybe he too had come to the belated realization that the commercials they'd argued over so vehemently weren't nearly as detrimental to their respective dealerships as they'd feared.

Lucky mulled that over with a frown. Did that mean that once business stopped being a bone of contention, there was nothing left to bring them together? Determinedly she pushed the notion aside. No, she'd been attracted to Sam and enjoyed his company, too. And unless she was crazy, he'd returned her interest full measure.

"Phooey!" Lucky muttered under her breath. Her fingers hooked the back of the phone and dragged it across the desk. If Sam wasn't going to call her, then she was just going to have to call him. That was all there was to it.

"Donahue Motors," a crisp voice answered on the first ring.

"Sam Donahue, please," Lucky said and gave her name.

In the minute it took for Sam to pick up his extension, she'd decided she was going to invite him to an auto fair that was taking place that weekend in Willow Grove. She'd been planning to go anyway; for all she knew, he was, too. Perhaps it was time to shift their relationship away from the arena of business, time to try spending a day on neutral ground and see what developed from there.

"Lucky?" Sam's voice came on the line. "I'm glad you called."

The moment she heard his voice, so was she. Their conversation was brief, but satisfying. In less than two minute's time, Lucky learned not only that Sam had spent the past three days at a symposium on marketing strategy in Wilmington, but that he had never been to an auto fair, and would be pleased to accompany her to this one.

"I'll pack a picnic lunch," she said, "and we can make a day of it."

"Perfect. I'll be looking forward to it."

One more step, Sam thought as he hung up the phone. With any luck, he'd figure out exactly where he was going before he got in too far over his head.

BY EIGHT-THIRTY Sunday morning Lucky had the Honda packed and ready to go. Since she hadn't arranged to pick up Sam until nine, that left her with approximately twenty minutes to kill. She used the time to change her outfit twice and her hairstyle three times—all while telling herself vehemently that she wasn't the slightest bit nervous about seeing Sam again.

When she reached his place, he was sitting outside, waiting. He rose as the Honda slid into a parking space, and Lucky's eyes slid up and down the length of his body appreciatively. Sam was dressed more casually than she'd seen him before, wearing khaki pants and a knit polo shirt that clung in all the right places. His body was lean and hard, the muscles firm without being bulky. He looked like a man who worked out to please himself and not because he wanted to make an impression on anyone else.

Because he was too far away to hear, she allowed herself a small, wistful sigh.

Sam walked around the passenger side and opened the door. Leaning down, he stuck his head inside. "Do you want me to drive?"

"Wouldn't dream of it," Lucky said with a grin. "I asked, I'm responsible."

"So that's how it works," Sam commented as he slid in beside her. "I always wondered."

"You have not." Lucky shifted deftly into reverse and maneuvered out of the space.

Remarkably, now that Sam was there, she found that her earlier nervousness had vanished. All that remained in its place was the sweet, simple joy of seeing him again. "Considering your looks, you've probably been dating since you were seven, and I've no doubt you had the whole thing figured out shortly thereafter."

"On the contrary, I was overweight as a child and wore glasses, to boot. I never made a single team in high school and barely managed a date for the senior prom."

Sam paused abruptly, his brow furrowing in surprise. He'd buried that self-conscious kid so deeply inside him that it had been years since he'd given him a thought. He'd never confessed his existence before, and certainly not to a woman. Now Sam tensed unconsciously, sure that he'd made a terrible mistake. The last thing he wanted was Lucky's pity.

A long moment passed before she replied, a moment during which Sam would have given a good deal more than the proverbial penny for her thoughts. "Is that why you don't have any pictures?" Lucky asked finally. "Because you didn't like the way you looked?"

"Partly, I suppose. Maybe even mostly. I knew even then that it wasn't a time in my life that I was going to remember fondly."

"And to think, you didn't even have any big brothers to defend you." Lucky turned and glanced his way. To his relief, Sam saw a wicked gleam in her eye. "Considering your inauspicious beginnings, I guess you turned out okay."

Sam felt the tension ease from his shoulders. He'd have hated having her feel sorry for him. Teasing, however, he could handle just fine. "Just okay?"

She slanted him a look. "I thought it was women who were supposed to fish for compliments."

"For a liberated lady, you sure have a lot of rules."

"Don't worry about it." Her smile was wide and amused. "I enjoy breaking them just as much as I enjoy making them."

"I'll remember that."

Sam drew the words out, as warm and slow as a caress. Though their seats were separated by at least a foot, Lucky

could have sworn he was touching her. It just wasn't possible for him to set the back of her neck tingling simply by
the tone of his voice. A quick glance in Sam's direction,
however, confirmed what she'd suspected. He was sitting
straight in his seat, his hands folded neatly in his lap.

She lifted her eyes, swallowed a breath, and didn't say
another word until she'd pulled off the turnpike at their exit.

"Tell me about this auto fair we're going to," Sam invited. "I take it it's not a new car show?"

"Not at all." The light turned green, and Lucky shifted
into first and shot around the corner. "All the cars you'll be
seeing today are used. Some are old enough to be considered antiques, but all of them are special in their own way.
For the most part, they're owned by car buffs who just can't
resist the chance to show them off."

"They'll be grouped by model—Mustangs in one row, for
example, Corvettes in another. Everybody who wants to
exhibit just pulls up and parks. Then they all get out and
walk around to see what everybody else has brought.
There's a competition, but mostly it's pretty low-key. The
majority of the owners are just there to show off, meet people with similar interests, and have a good time."

Obviously Lucky's idea of a good time and his differed
dramatically, Sam thought, staring out the side window.
When she'd called, he'd accepted her invitation eagerly. He
wanted to see her again; it was as simple as that. At the time,
he'd paid little attention to where their date was going to
take them. If anything, she'd made the idea of an auto fair
seem mildly intriguing.

But the more he knew about what it entailed, the less ex-
citing the prospect sounded. He'd go along because that was
what Lucky wanted to do. But beyond that, he had no intention of faking an enthusiasm he was far from feeling.

At the gate, Lucky paid admission for the two of them, then steered her Honda into the parking lot. Sam had been very quiet since she'd explained the nature of the day's outing and now, as they climbed from the car, she wondered whether inviting him had been a good idea.

Though she'd told herself she'd done so for the pleasure of his company, Lucky was forced to admit that she'd also had an ulterior motive. It was about time someone shook up those preconceived notions of his just a little. He needed to be shown that things didn't have to be new in order to possess beauty or value. And if the task fell to her, well, so be it.

"This way." Lucky steered him over to the larger field where colorful flags and banners marked the rows of cars. "They seem to be grouped in alphabetical order. Name your pleasure."

"No, you pick," Sam insisted. "After all, you're the one who's in charge."

"Fords," Lucky announced decisively, striding away.

It took Sam a hurried step to catch up, time that he spent appreciating the zeal with which Lucky had once again thrown herself into whatever the moment had to offer. "Any particular reason why?"

"Lots." She glanced up and grinned. "Mustangs and Thunderbirds for starters. And every so often, you get lucky and an Edsel shows up."

Wonderful, thought Sam. As if there was anything to be admired about one of the most colossal mistakes in automotive history. Then again, he reflected, his gaze scanning the field, at least an Edsel might prove mildly interesting, which was more than could be said for the rest of the fair. From what he could see, it looked like nothing more than an organized version of the hot-rod rallies he'd avoided so studiously in high school.

Hanging back, Sam was content to let Lucky take the lead. Eyes wide, she wandered from one exhibit to the next, stopping every so often to admire a two-tone paint job or a set of mag wheels. Watching her, Sam discovered that she was just as likely to poke her head under the hood of a '66 Camaro as she was to hunker down and examine the bicycle thin tires of a Model T Ford.

She talked to the owners and asked questions, tons of them. Whether the men responded to the lithe femininity of her figure or the appeal of her eager curiosity, Sam couldn't be sure. All he knew was that in no time flat she'd been accepted into the circle of exhibitors, her opinions sought and given as freely as their own.

With a pang of something—certainly not jealousy, Sam told himself firmly—he watched her impress the drivers with her charm and intelligence. For the second time that morning, he found himself remembering the fat, fourteen-year-old boy who'd been excluded from cliques just like these. Remembering, and not liking it a bit.

By eleven o'clock Lucky was beginning to realize the magnitude of her error. By noon she'd passed that stage and was beginning to grow irritated. Maybe Sam was never planning to speak again, she groused silently as she trailed her fingers appreciatively over the shiny new paint job of a huge old Chrysler Imperial. Indeed, if the last hour was anything to go by, maybe he'd lost his voice entirely.

She'd done her best to pique his interest and get him involved. She'd acted as guide and impromptu emcee both, showing him everything from Cadillacs to Carmen Ghias. And through it all, he managed to remain aloof, his eyes bored, his expression faintly disapproving. When she talked to the owners, he hung back. More than once, she'd addressed a question in his direction, only to turn and find him staring absently off into the distance. Whatever it was he was looking for, Lucky reflected, it was a cinch he didn't plan on finding it at the auto show.

It was with an air of resigned disappointment that she finally suggested they go back to the Honda and get their lunch. All around them, families were laying out their picnics, and Lucky whispered a silent plea that the day not turn out to be a total disaster. If Sam wasn't going to enjoy the cars, then maybe, just maybe, he'd enjoy the food.

They found a spot beneath a huge, leafy elm. Lucky spread out an old army blanket, a veteran of many such outings, then sat down and unpacked the food. She waited until Sam had helped himself to a chunk of French bread, several slices of baked ham and a wedge of Brie; waited until he'd opened the wine and poured a glass for them both; waited until he'd plucked a fresh grape from the bunch, popped it into his mouth and chewed blissfully. And then she demanded an explanation.

"Tell me what I'm doing wrong."

Sam glanced up, surprised. "You? Nothing."

Lucky's frown held more than a hint of exasperation. "You're having a terrible time. I want to know why."

"I am not," Sam began automatically, then stopped. It was amazing how easily she seemed to read his moods. Disconcerting, too. Most of the women he'd known had been far too involved in their own enjoyment to worry about someone else's. Yet, to all appearances, Lucky seemed seriously concerned about the way he was feeling.

"Don't forget, I have brothers," she warned. "I can recognize a convenient lie at sixty paces."

"I wouldn't say that I'm having a terrible time, exactly..."

Lucky helped herself to a hunk of bread and slathered it with butter. "Exactly what would you call it, then?"

Sam struggled for the words, trying to find a way to explain. "I look around here, and I feel like a fish out of water. My frame of reference is totally different. Take that man with the '54 Chevy Coupe."

Her mouth full, Lucky settled for a nod.

"All he could talk about was how many times he'd pulled out the engine and rebuilt it. And to top it off, he didn't seem to think he'd gotten the damn thing right yet!"

"It wasn't that he didn't have it right. Older things just require more care, that's all."

"Exactly," said Sam. "So if he likes the car so much, why doesn't he just put in a new engine that actually runs and be done with it?"

"You're missing the point. It's precisely because he likes the car that he doesn't want to tamper with its integrity. Once he put in a new engine, it would never be the same."

"Tamper with its integrity?" Sam choked on a laugh. "These are cars we're discussing, not presidential candidates."

"I thought you were interested in cars." Lucky made no attempt to hide her irritation. "That's why I asked you to come in the first place. But of course that was before I realized that you were too much of a snob to relax and enjoy yourself."

Sam thought the gulf between them had never felt so wide. He might have envied Lucky's easy camaraderie with the drivers at the show, but even if he'd wanted to, he hadn't a clue as to how to emulate it. He'd always been a bit of a loner, always preferred it that way. But that didn't make him a snob.

"Admit it," said Lucky. "The real reason you can't get interested in these cars is because they're not fresh off the boat from Europe, complete with plastic sheeting over their seats and huge sticker prices."

"That's unfair."

"Is it?"

Sam began to gather up the picnic things and stow them in the basket. "The next time you're mooning over one of those two-tone Chevys, try taking a closer look. There's nothing noble about cracked vinyl seats or an interior that will never smell like anything but stale cigarette butts. If wanting something a little better, a little newer, makes me a snob, so be it. But I've never seen anything wrong with wanting the best and striving hard to get it."

They finished repacking the picnic basket in silence. While Lucky carried it back to the car, Sam gathered up the garbage and tossed it in the bin. "Do you want to leave?" Lucky asked when they met at the edge of the lot.

"We're here now." Sam sounded resigned. "We may as well see the rest of them."

Lucky had dragged little brothers to the dentist who'd shown more enthusiasm. But if Sam thought she'd do the gracious thing and insist they leave, he was wrong. It was a beautiful day to be outside and, Sam's participation aside, she was enjoying the auto fair enormously. If he didn't like it, that was just too bad.

The first row they explored after lunch contained four-wheel-drive vehicles. The next held sedans, most unless Sam missed his guess, circa nineteen-sixty. As Lucky paused to comment appreciatively on a Ford Fairlane, he wandered on ahead. At the end of the row, he turned automatically to start up the next, then stopped dead.

Sitting in front of him was, if not the most beautiful piece of machinery he'd ever seen, certainly a car that came close—a 1960 Rolls Royce Silver Shadow, its taupe and tan exterior set off by huge headlamps and a gleaming grill, the familiar winged ornament perched proudly on the hood.

For a moment, he could only stare. Then, drawn inexorably, he moved in for a closer look.

"Pretty, isn't she?"

Sam turned as the speaker came up beside him. "Only to a blind man. Anyone else would say she was gorgeous. Yours?"

The man nodded.

"Mind if I take a look inside?"

"Be my guest."

The door slid open with a smooth, well oiled precision that spoke volumes about the superior craftsmanship of the car. Sam leaned his head inside and inhaled the scent of leather, strong and fresh. The mahogany dashboard shone with the polished patina of fine old wood. The clock, made before the days of digitals, still ticked after almost thirty years. The instrument panel was old-fashioned, but in many ways still wonderfully familiar.

Sam straightened and, with a smile, began to ask questions.

Lucky found him there twenty minutes later. The moment she'd rounded the corner, she'd seen the car that had caught his eye. A Rolls Royce, of course. But what a car it was. Lucky strolled in closer, sidled up to where Sam and the owner were talking and found she could hardly get a word in edgewise.

She could have been miffed, but *pleased* came closer to the mark. That, and perhaps a bit smug. Maybe the day wasn't totally lost after all.

"I was beginning to think I was going to have to tie you up and drag you away," Lucky teased forty-five minutes later when Sam was finally ready to move on.

"You were the one who wanted me to get involved."

"You're right," Lucky agreed. "I'm glad you finally found something that captured your interest."

"That Rolls was more than interesting, it was a work of art."

"Even though it was old?"

"Age has nothing to do with it," Sam began, then paused. "Do I hear a lecture coming?"

"From me?" Lucky smiled sweetly. "Of course not."

"Funny, I could have sworn you were about to say I told you so."

"I never gloat. Even when, as frequently happens, I'm right."

"Don't press your luck," Sam warned, his voice low and amused. "Or I might be forced to remind you how many Fords and Chevys we had to sort through before we found a car that was really worth seeing."

Lucky tilted her nose in the air. "Beauty is in the eye of the beholder."

"Precisely, and some of these babies only a mother could love."

She covered a chuckle by clearing her throat hastily. She was supposed to be making Sam see things her way. But could she help it if she was beginning to see the merit in his position as well? "I guess you're entitled to your opinion."

"I'm glad to hear you say that, because—"

Abruptly conversation stopped as they rounded the end of the last row and came unexpectedly upon a small girl standing all alone by the side of a car. She was clutching a tattered stuffed dog to her chest and sniffling loudly. At their approach, the child looked up hopefully. In the span of a second, hope turned to tears, however, and she began to wail. Immediately Lucky dropped to her knees to face the girl at her own level.

"Are you lost?" she asked.

The little girl nodded, lower lip quivering.

"Do you want us to help you find your parents?"

The child thought for a moment, then drew a deep breath. "I'm not allowed to talk to strangers," she announced.

"You're very smart to know that," Lucky agreed solemnly. "But just this one time, I think it might be all right to make an exception. What do you think?"

"I don't know. . . ."

"I'll tell you what, maybe it will be all right if we don't talk about you. Tell me about your dog. Does he have a name?"

Shyly, the little girl nodded. She looked down at the stuffed animal she held in her arms, then back to Lucky. Finally some sort of decision seemed to have been made for she held the puppy out to Lucky and said, "His name is Fluffy. Would you like to hold him?"

Sam watched in silence as Lucky took the stuffed dog and cradled it gently in her arms. No wonder she was so good at selling used cars, he mused. The more he saw of Lucky, the more he realized it was a good thing she hadn't gotten it into her head to start selling shares in the Brooklyn Bridge. Undoubtedly, if she had, there'd be plenty of takers.

Lucky's way of developing an instant rapport with everyone she met was nothing short of amazing. She was so open, so genuinely caring, that people just couldn't seem to help responding in kind—even this frightened four-year-old, who was now sitting in Lucky's lap and chattering away happily.

Sam realized he'd have been at a loss to deal with the situation without Lucky's intervention. He'd always been uncomfortable around children, an uneasiness he'd blamed on a lack of familiarity. But understanding the problem wouldn't have been much help if he'd been the one who had to cope.

He'd have had no idea how to make the little girl stop crying, much less how to elicit the necessary information to reunite her with her parents. Yet Lucky had managed the whole thing effortlessly, as though her actions were nothing special at all.

There was a certain clarity to the thought that struck him then, as he stood by the edge of the field, the hot noonday sun beating down on his head, the sounds of the fair eddying around him in the humid summer air. Whether she realized it or not, Lucky Vanderholden *was* special. She was the kind of woman who, by her very presence, would make a difference in the lives of those around her.

She was going to make a difference in his life, too. Of that, Sam was certain. The knowledge, sudden and sure, was as unnerving as it was intriguing.

## 6

"LET'S HEAD OVER to the loudspeaker," Lucky suggested. "I'm sure they'll be happy to make an announcement."

"What?" Sam glanced up, pulled from his thoughts. "Oh, right."

Within minutes, the little girl had been reunited with her worried parents. Lucky's gaze followed the happy family as they walked away. "I guess we may as well be going, too," she said when they'd disappeared. "We've seen just about everything."

"Just *about* everything?" Sam teased as they started toward the car. "Despite the size of that field, I don't think we missed a single square inch."

"It pays to be thorough. Just think, if we'd given up after lunch, you'd never have seen that Rolls."

"Somehow, I'm quite certain I'd have survived."

"Sure," Lucky said easily. "But what about me? I liked watching you fall in love with something old and beautiful. Maybe your finer instincts aren't defunct, after all."

Sam's hand reached around to deliver a playful swat, but Lucky saw his intention and eluded him nimbly. She tossed back her curls and flashed him an impudent grin. "Although your reflexes don't seem to be what they used to be."

"Are you calling me old?"

"Of course not—just slow."

"I'll show you slow!" Sam threatened, and Lucky took off across the lot. Within seconds, he was flying after her.

How long had it been since he'd flirted with a woman? Sam wondered. How long since he'd given himself up to the simple enjoyment of another person's company? But it wasn't just anyone he wanted beside him, Sam realized, racing along after her. Only Lucky. Her presence acted like a powerful drug to his system, heightening his awareness, fine-tuning his reactions, until it seemed as though his life had gained a vibrancy, an urgency, he'd never felt before.

When she ducked between the last row of cars, Sam was right behind her. He waited until she'd reached the Honda then, laughing, caught her there, his arms reaching around either side to trap her between him and the car.

"You lost," Lucky informed him smugly. Eyes dancing, she tilted her head at a cocky angle, enjoying her victory enormously.

To Sam, she'd never been more beautiful. "Oh, I don't know," he said softly. "I'd say that's all in how you look at things."

Sam's smile was so warm, so filled with tenderness that without thinking, Lucky lifted a finger to trace the smooth outline of his lips. His tongue flicked out, catching her by surprise, and she raised startled eyes to his. Abruptly her hands stilled.

In a single step Sam fit Lucky into his arms. Lucky's fingertips braced against his chest, and for an uncertain moment, she wondered whether she meant to draw him close or push him away. Then her fingers curled into the soft cotton fabric, grasping and holding. As Sam's head came down, she rose on her toes to meet him.

The solid thrust of his tongue in her mouth sent a spear of sensation racing to her core. She felt the warmth of the sun overhead mingling with the fiery yearning from within. Need rose inside her, a molten force that flowed through her veins until all her nerve endings seemed to tingle with desire.

And still the kiss went on and on. Sam held Lucky to him, possessed by a hunger and eagerness that was stunning in its urgency. There was an incredible feeling of rightness to holding her in his arms, a symmetry to the way her body molded to his own.

His hand slid up over her rib cage, then stopped just below her breast. Lucky leaned into him with a moan that came from deep within her throat. But before Sam could respond, he became dimly aware of another sound—approaching footsteps and the babble of conversation, growing steadily louder. Gradually, consciousness of their surroundings returned. With it came a sense of shock at how quickly, how deeply, he'd lost himself within her.

Shaken, flushed, Sam eased back to put some distance between them. Through half-lowered lids, he took in Lucky's appearance. Her lips were pink and slightly swollen, the look on her face, dazed. He drew a deep breath, holding it until he was sure he'd regained control.

"Sorry," he said raggedly. "I didn't mean for that to happen."

"That's funny." Lucky gave her head a faint shake. "I could have sworn you were the one who kissed me."

"*That* I meant. I just didn't think things would get out of hand so quickly."

Sam's eyes were dark and still smoldering, his lips curved in a rueful smile. With a start, Lucky realized that right at that very moment, she wanted nothing more than to pull him into her arms and kiss him all over again—even if they *were* standing in the middle of a parking lot in broad daylight.

There was only one way she could possibly deal with such a notion, and that was to pretend that it didn't exist. "You don't look like the kind of man who's in the habit of apologizing for kissing a woman," Lucky said briskly. Edging past Sam, she walked around to her door.

"You're right," he replied as they both climbed in. "I'm not.

"Then don't start now."

Lucky reached forward to fit the key into the ignition. As she started to turn it Sam's hand came out to cover hers, holding it still. "Let's not go back yet," he said. "You've entertained me today. I'd like to do the same for you tonight. Have dinner with me."

"I can't."

"Maybe I haven't been the best of company," Sam was surprised by his need to explain, to ensure that their time together didn't end just yet. He rushed on before she was able to refuse. "But tonight will be different. We'll do something that has nothing to do with cars. We won't look at them, won't talk about them—"

"No really," Lucky broke in. "I can't. I have other plans."

"I see."

From the angry set of his shoulders, it was clear to Lucky that he didn't see at all. He suspected she'd arranged another date for that evening, and nothing could be further from the truth. "I'm getting together with my family."

"Marete?" When Lucky shook her head, Sam tried again. "Ken?"

"Hal," Lucky supplied with a grin. "My newlywed brother. He and his wife are having a barbecue tonight for the whole family. Betty loves to cook and doesn't appear to be at all daunted by the Vanderholden hordes. In fact . . ." Lucky paused for a moment to think. "Since you're not doing anything, why don't you join us? At Hal's house, there's always room for one more."

"I couldn't possibly," Sam said quickly.

"Why not? You just said you weren't busy."

"Yes, but . . ."

"Chicken?"

"Of course not!"

"Good, then it's settled." Lucky turned the key in the ignition and the engine began to hum. Smiling to herself, she pictured the evening to come. The Incredible Hunk meets the Brady Bunch. If nothing else, it was going to be interesting.

SAM WONDERED what he had gotten himself into. Standing beside the keg that had been set up in Hal and Betty's backyard, he sipped at a long, cold beer and gazed around avidly. He'd known Lucky's family was large, but somehow he hadn't expected the gathering to be quite so . . . overwhelming.

People filled the small raised deck and spilled out onto the patio below. The yard, already crowded with tables and chairs, absorbed the rest of the overflow, most of whom seemed to be gathered around what had to be the biggest barbecue pit Sam had ever seen.

Upon their arrival, Lucky had performed the introductions. Using skills honed during his salesman days, Sam had managed to commit the first two dozen names to memory. After that, he'd had to give up, and could only hope that Lucky would stay by his side to help him sort people out.

It was a good idea in theory. And it had worked well until one of Lucky's sisters—Isabel, he thought—had grabbed Lucky's arm and dragged her toward the kitchen where a group of Vanderholden women were immersed in the plans for an upcoming family wedding. Left to his own devices, Sam had gone over to the keg and drawn a draft, then leaned back against the maple tree that shaded it to enjoy the beer and spend some time in quiet observation.

It didn't take Sam long to realize, however, that a number of Lucky's relatives were observing him with a degree of interest that rivaled his own. Not only that, but if the open stares he was receiving were any indication, subtlety was not a Vanderholden virtue. All at once he had a fair idea of how a deer felt on the first day of hunting season.

A movement caught the corner of his eye, and Sam ducked just in time to avoid being hit by a Frisbee that slammed into the tree trunk behind him, then bounced away. A tow-haired boy of about eight came flying after it, then stopped when he saw Sam.

"Yours?" Sam crouched down to retrieve the bright red disc.

"Yeah." The boy ducked his head.

"What do you say, Brad?" a man's voice asked. Sam looked up to see one of Lucky's brothers standing above them. Frank, the second oldest, unless he missed his guess.

"I'm glad it didn't hit you, mister."

"That's not what I mean," Frank said sternly.

"I'm sorry, it won't happen again."

"And?"

"Thanks!" Frisbee in hand, Brad was off like a shot.

Sam straightened to face the boy's father. "He's a cute kid."

"Sometimes," Frank acknowledged. He refilled his mug at the tap. "And sometimes he's a pain in the—"

"Frank!" said a woman, coming up behind them. "Don't you dare! You'll give Sam the wrong idea." She turned to Sam, held out her hand and flashed him a friendly smile. "Hi, I'm Marete. I was in the kitchen when you arrived."

"Ah yes. You're the cake maker."

Marete shrugged. "The instigator, anyway. Lucky's the one who can actually bake."

Sam remembered what Lucky had said about her older sister's propensity to matchmake and held back a grin.

"Watch out for her," Ken warned in a stage whisper, as he came up to join them. "Marete is the organizer. Don't admit to having any skills or she'll put you to work."

"You won't need skill," Marete told her little brother sweetly. "I'm sure when clean-up time comes, there'll be plenty of manual labor to go around."

"See what I mean?" Ken rolled his eyes.

"I'd be happy to help out—" Sam began.

"But not just yet," Frank interrupted. "Sam's a guest, and he's just arrived. We haven't even had a chance to talk."

"How's everybody doing?" asked Hal. He looked around the circle as he drew a refill of beer.

"Fine," Ken said with a grin. "Frank's about to give Lucky's date the third degree."

"Hush!" Marete leveled her brother a look. "Nobody asked your opinion."

"Well you have to admit it isn't every day that Lucky brings somebody home—"

"Ken," Frank broke in quickly. "Isn't that Mom's voice I hear calling you?"

"I don't hear anything."

"Sure you do," Marete's hand, applied firmly to the middle of Ken's back, hastened him along. "Why don't you go inside and see?"

With effort, Sam kept a straight face at Ken's obvious disgruntlement. Seeing the Vanderholdens in action, he could well understand where Lucky had gotten her persuasive skills. Singly, they were hard to resist. As a group, they were nothing short of formidable.

Frank turned back to Sam as Ken walked away. "So, how did you and my sister meet?"

By the time Lucky reappeared, the group near the keg had joined those around the barbecue. A lively debate was in progress concerning the amount of time it took to flame broil the perfect hamburger. When Sam's natural reticence would have made him hang back, the Vanderholdens' enthusiasm rendered such reserve all but impossible. They might be curious about him, but they were also, by nature, a warm and caring group. In no time at all, Sam found himself accepted into their midst like a long-lost relative.

Now, watching the family interact, Sam realized that Lucky's siblings enjoyed a unique brand of closeness that was unlike anything he had ever known. Even their disagreements were settled efficiently, and with no loss of good humor. And despite the confusion that reigned supreme, the tables still managed to get set and the dinner prepared.

"How are you holding up?" Lucky asked as she and Sam moved down the buffet table, piling their plates high with food.

"Fine, I think. Although if one more person tries to sound me out on my intentions, I won't be responsible for the consequences."

"They haven't really been doing that." Lucky sounded unconvinced. "Have they?"

"In spades." Sam spooned a general helping of pasta salad onto his plate. "Why are you so surprised? You told me yourself Marete was trying to marry you off."

"I know. It's just that I was hoping they might display a little more tact, especially since I spent a good ten minutes in the kitchen threatening mayhem to anyone who didn't."

Sam glanced over in surprise, touched by her efforts on his behalf. "Thanks for the thought, but in case you're interested, Frank and Hal seemed to have missed the lecture. Betty and Marete may have heard it, but they're not paying much attention."

"We'll just see about that."

Sam recognized the devilish gleam in her eye. In the past, it had left him grappling with slanderous commercials and chocolate fudge cakes. "What are you going to do?"

"You'll see." Lucky set down her plate and picked up an empty glass. As Sam watched, she pulled out a chair and climbed up on top of it. Tapping the side of the glass with a spoon, she called out loudly, "Excuse me everyone! Can I have your attention please?"

It took a moment, but gradually the noise died down. One by one, heads turned to see what Lucky was up to.

"I have an announcement to make. It has come to my attention that many of you are curious as to why Sam Donahue is here tonight. For those of you who are interested, there are two reasons. One—he is my friend and neighbor, no more, no less. And two . . ." she paused, waiting for total silence. "We were hungry!"

Amid much hooting and catcalling Lucky climbed back down. Seemingly unaware of Sam's incredulous gaze, she set down the glass and spoon and picked up her plate once more. "I can't believe you just did that," he managed finally.

"Why not?"

"Do you really think making an announcement like that is going to stop all the speculation?"

"Of course not," Lucky said easily. "Actually, it will probably make it worse. But now, nobody will dare to bother you. They'll come to me instead."

"And then what?"

"Don't worry about me. I've been dealing with my family for years."

He'd never thought of unpredictability as an asset before, Sam mused as they gathered up their silverware and headed toward one of the other tables to sit down. But now he was discovering that he found himself as charmed by Lucky's penchant for doing the unexpected as he had by her sensitivity with the little girl they'd found at the fair.

Lucky seemed not at all concerned that her outrageous pronouncement had the effect of turning all eyes at the gathering surreptitiously in their direction. With her head high and her shoulders squared, she led the way to the picnic table at the end. At their approach, conversation at the table waned. Lucky set down her plate with an attention-getting thump.

"Behave yourselves," she warned. "There's a guest present." Turning to Sam, she added in a deliberately loud aside. "I can't help it. I've done all I can. They mean well, but they really are about the nosiest bunch of people you'll ever meet."

"I resent that!" Hal cried as Sam and Lucky slid into the last two seats.

"You may," Lucky shot back. "But I don't hear you denying it."

At once the conversation was off and running again as those at the table threw themselves into the argument with gusto. Content to let the discussion eddy around him, Sam found that he had eyes only for Lucky. Slowly, inexorably, she was putting him under her spell. If she could leave him feeling this thoroughly bewitched at a noisy gathering, who knew what might be possible when they had a chance to be alone...."

"Smile!"

Sam glanced up and found himself staring down the lens of a camera held by a young pixie of a woman standing at the end of the table. "What now?" he asked. "Mug shots?"

"I guess you haven't met Janice." Lucky paused to smile as a flashbulb went off in the semi-darkness around them.

"She's the self-appointed family chronicler. Jan never goes anywhere without her camera."

"That's fine for a group shot," Lucky's sister declared. "Now how about a few of the couples?"

Amid much good-natured grumbling, everyone rearranged themselves by family. Rather than waiting for her subjects to pose, Janice caught them in the act of being themselves. Hal was captured waving an ear of corn with mock menace under Betty's nose. Lucky's parents were snapped in the midst of a surreptitious kiss. When Lucky and Sam's turn came, he got into the spirit of things by sliding an arm around her waist to pull her close, then tickling her unmercifully as the shutter snapped.

Janice considered Sam as she wound her film, then slipped Lucky a sly wink. "He'll do," she pronounced before moving on.

Lucky had to laugh at the look on Sam's face. "I tried to warn you. Where my family is concerned, there's almost no such thing as privacy."

"So I see. I started with one Vanderholden, but now suddenly I'm beginning to feel as though I'm dating the entire family."

"Don't worry. With any luck, we'll have ourselves back down to manageable numbers soon."

Sam looked around at the gathering skeptically. "Do you really think all these people are going to clear out anytime soon?"

"No . . ." Lucky's voice dropped several octaves, going warm and husky with promise. "But we might."

Like the rest of her relatives, she'd been watching him all evening. But unlike them, there'd been no curiosity in her gaze, only pure, unadulterated appreciation. She'd thrust Sam into a potentially uncomfortable situation, and he'd handled himself with aplomb. She, more than anyone, knew how intimidating her family could be. And though she'd done her best to shield him, in the end, her efforts had proven unnecessary.

As always, Sam had been smooth, polite, and very much in control. It was exactly that thought that made her tingle with anticipation as she contemplated the delicious prospect of having Sam all to herself. She wanted to hold him in her arms and strip away the polished veneer he presented to the world, to feel him tremble beneath her touch as he had earlier. And most of all, right at that moment, she wanted to be anywhere else but there.

Lucky's fingertips skated the length of Sam's arm. "Of course if you'd rather stay...?"

Sam's reply to that was a low, sexy laugh that gave Lucky's pulse rate a boost. Ten minutes later, by mutual agreement, they'd made their goodbyes and were on their way. When they reached Sam's apartment, he didn't bother to ask whether she was coming in. Instead, he simply walked around, opened her door, and took her hand in his.

"Would you like something to drink?" he asked, once they were inside.

"Coffee?"

"Sure." While the coffee brewed, Sam set a tray with cups and saucers. At the last minute, he opened a cabinet and pulled out a bag of Oreo cookies. He offered them to Lucky, then popped one in his mouth before picking up their cups and heading into the living room.

"You'll get crumbs on your couch," she said as she sank down into the plush leather cushion.

"Only if you're a messy eater." Sam set the tray on the table, and promptly forgot it. After an entire day of running around, he finally had Lucky all to himself and eating was the last thing on his mind.

Beside him, Lucky picked up her spoon and stirred her coffee with a vengeance. She'd looked forward to being alone with Sam. But now that it had happened, now that they were actually sitting side by side on his couch, her confidence had fled leaving only a dry mouth and clammy palms in its wake. All at once conversation seemed like a safer bet than any of the other options that came to mind.

"Well," Lucky said brightly. "Now you've met my whole family. What do you think?"

"I think that I don't want to talk about them."

"That bad?"

"No," Sam said softly. "At the moment, just unimportant."

"Oh." Lucky lifted her cup to her lips. The coffee was hot and scalded her tongue. With a clatter, she set the cup back in its saucer.

"Lucky?"

"Hmm?"

"Are you all right?"

"Fine." Her voice broke on a squeak.

"So I see." The corner of Sam's mouth quirked as he reached out and took the cup and saucer from her hands and set it on the table.

The casual touch of Sam's fingers across her own was enough to set Lucky's pulse racing. All at once her nervousness fled as far stronger emotions rose to take its place. For weeks, she and Sam had been sparring and igniting sparks. And for weeks the attraction had been building until suddenly it was hard to think of anything else but the emptiness in the pit of her stomach, an emptiness that could only be assuaged by the feeling of Sam's arms wrapped around her.

Lucky gazed upward, her eyes wide. "What happens next?"

Sam slid across the seat until their legs were touching from thigh to knee. He lifted one hand to her face, gently stroking the smooth slope of her cheek, then tangled his fingers in her hair. "You know the answer to that."

She did, but she wanted to hear it, anyway. "Tell me."

"Next," Sam murmured, "I'm going to kiss you."

Slowly he touched his mouth to hers. His lips were warm and soft and tasted faintly of chocolate. Their pressure was firm, the touch electrifying. In the space of an instant, Lucky felt her heart begin to pound.

How could desire flare so quickly? she wondered. How could wants turn to needs with a man she hardly knew at all, a man with whom she'd spent more time as adversary than friend? In the past her passion had built slowly, growing naturally as a relationship progressed. Yet what she felt now bore no more relation to that pale emotion than a brushfire did to a match.

With a small sigh, Lucky pushed the questions aside. Her lips parted, and Sam's tongue entered her mouth, sliding in possessively with a tantalizing lack of haste. She wanted this, oh how she wanted this. And maybe, for now, that was all she need to know.

Sam's hand drifted downward through her curls, then stroked the smooth column of her throat. His fingertips feathered lightly over the arch of her collarbone. Responding to the gentle pressure, Lucky sank back into the soft cushions, then reached up to pull Sam down beside her.

With a small groan, Sam adjusted his weight to cover her body with his own. She felt so good beneath him, as though her body had been fashioned for the express purpose of matching his. He'd seen Lucky's hesitation and realized she had doubts. But now, as they lay together, her hips were moving in a rhythm that timed with his, and when his palm settled over her breast, she gave a small gasp of pleasure before her hand covered his and pressed him closer. She seemed stunned by the passionate depths of her own response . . . and still just the tiniest bit unsure.

With a hoarse breath, Sam lifted himself away. He watched as Lucky's eyes opened slowly, her gaze dreamy and unfocused. She reached for him, then hesitated, her hand coming to rest on his arm. "What's the matter?"

"This isn't right."

"I don't understand." Lucky struggled to sit up amidst the soft cushions that seemed to conspire to hold her within their depths. "I thought you . . . I thought we—" she paused, then sent the words out in a rush "—wanted each other."

Sam groaned softly. "I want you, Lucky. I want you so badly I ache. But what I don't want is to seduce you. I want the timing, the feelings, to be right for both of us."

Lucky succeeded in sitting up, as frowning, she considered what Sam had said. She couldn't argue with him because it was true. She *had* been seduced—by Sam's quick mind and his ready wit, by his long, lean body and his smoky gray eyes. But it was true as well that she'd had her reservations.

Sam was different from the men she'd had relationships with in the past, men with whom she'd been friends first and lovers later. She'd been comfortable with them, secure. And if the sparks that had flown between them had seemed more pleasant than earth-shattering, well, she'd told herself that was just the way things were.

But now, with Sam, nothing seemed to be going quite the way she'd expected. He'd challenged her mentally. Physically, he was more than capable of making her head spin. And emotionally . . . ? Lucky supposed that remained to be seen.

With a token show of dignity, she concentrated on straightening her clothes. If she'd ever taken up smoking, now would have been the perfect time for a cigarette. In lieu of that, Lucky reached for a cookie. She chewed slowly, then washed the Oreo down with a sip of tepid coffee.

"I've never known anyone quite like you before," she said finally.

Sam's brow rose. "Is that good or bad?"

"That's the problem. I don't know you well enough to say."

"That can be fixed."

"Yes," Lucky agreed, her lips curved in a half smile. "It can."

With his fingertips, Sam traced the soft outline of her smile. "How you tempt me," he muttered.

"Is that what I'm doing?"

Her eyelashes fluttered, and unexpectedly Sam found himself grinning at the blatantly seductive look she had plastered across her face. The last of the awkwardness that had hovered between them vanished.

"You also try my patience," he mentioned, rising to his feet.

"Good." Lucky stood as well.

"Good?"

"A little turmoil is good for the soul. It shakes you up, keeps you on your toes."

"Of course," Sam said blandly. "Everyone should have some."

"Come on," Lucky scoffed, poking him in the ribs. "You love it."

They laughed together then, and a few minutes later, Sam escorted Lucky out to her car. But as he stood in the driveway and watched her taillights disappear in the night, he was still pondering her comment. The worst part was, he had a sneaking suspicion she was right.

"SHE'S DONE IT AGAIN!"

Sam stormed into the showroom, a copy of the afternoon's paper clutched in his hand.

Joe Saks, Donahue Motors' senior salesman, looked up from the figures he was going over at his desk. "She who?"

"Lucky Vanderholden, who else?"

"What's she done?"

Sam's glare held all the warmth of granite in winter. "Dreamed up another crazy promotional scheme, that's what! Look at this."

The paper sliced through the air and landed on Joe's desk, scattering his tidy pile of invoices. Ignoring them, Joe cast his gaze obediently downward to check out the headline. "'Philadelphia zoo adopts orphan tiger.' What's that got to do with—"

"Not there," Sam snapped. "Here!" His finger pointed to a gaudy ad that took up a full quarter of the page.

Joe scanned it quickly and looked up. "It's an announcement for a spring carnival. So what?"

"Keep going."

"'Come one, come all,'" Joe read aloud. "'Clowns, games, rides and plenty of excitement. Fun for the whole family...'" He frowned quizzically. "I still don't see—"

"Check out the address," Sam said with barely concealed impatience. He leaned over and read the ad's offending last line for himself. "To be held at 689 Front Street, home of Lucky's Late-Model Lovelies." He rolled his eyes heavenward. "She's actually planning to hold this extravaganza right next door!"

"So it would seem." Joe looked down to inspect the fine print.

"She can't be serious," Sam said after a moment. Even to his own ears, his voice lacked conviction.

"The lady sells used cars for a living, Sam. A big splashy promotion like this is probably right up her alley."

"Surely she must realize something that size is bound to turn the whole neighborhood upside down."

Joe looked up and shrugged. "Maybe she doesn't mind."

"We'll just see about that!" Sam spun on his heel and headed for the door.

"If we need you for anything . . . ?" Joe called after him.

"Call next door!"

If things kept up like this much longer, he was going to have to cut a gate in the damned fence, Sam thought irritably as he strode outside and set out toward the road.

In the three days since he'd last seen Lucky, she'd never been far from his thoughts. Even at work, where his formidable powers of concentration had always before provided a refuge against outside distractions, her image had hovered, gossamerlike, on the fringes of his imagination.

A dozen times he'd found his hand straying toward the telephone, and a dozen times he'd made the conscious decision to haul it back. Lucky needed more time to get used to what was happening between them. He'd seen that for himself Sunday night. And perhaps, if the truth be told, so did he. Time to come to grips with the unexpectedly strong feelings she aroused within him. Time to examine the course of their relationship and decide where they were going from here.

As Sam's long, swinging stride carried him around the corner and onto Lucky's lot, his thoughts returned to the upcoming carnival, and he frowned grimly. Then again, there was always the chance that they weren't going anywhere. At least not until they got a few things straightened out!

LUCKY WAS IN the small garage behind her office when she first became aware that something was amiss. She'd been talking to her mechanic, Clem Greeley, but when Sam strode through the open door like an Indian on the warpath, their conversation abruptly died.

"Sam," Lucky began. "What a pleasant surprise."

"No, it's not." Sam grasped her arm and pulled her toward the office door. "I want to talk to you. Now."

"Wait just a minute," said Clem. He didn't like the look on Sam's face, any more than he liked the proprietary way the man had seized his boss's arm.

"It's all right," Lucky reassured him quickly. "Sam and I are friends."

"He don't look too friendly to me."

Privately Lucky had to agree, but for Clem's sake, she pretended all was well. "Clem, this is Sam Donahue. He owns the dealership next door. Sam, Clem Greeley, my mechanic."

Reluctantly the two men shook hands.

"If you don't mind," Sam said with forced politeness, "there are a few things you and I need to discuss."

"Of course." Lucky turned to Clem. "We were just about finished anyway, weren't we?"

The older man nodded. He watched, his eyes narrowed, as Sam and Lucky headed toward the door. "You need any help, Lucky, you just call out. I'll be right there."

"Thank you, Clem." Lucky glanced back and sent the mechanic a smile of genuine affection. "I'm sure everything will be fine." Then the door that connected the garage to the office swung shut behind them, and she turned to Sam with a glare. "What was that all about? I'd never have guessed that cavemen tactics were part of your retinue."

"They're not," Sam said with a frown.

Immediately he released Lucky's arm and was shocked to see that his fingers had left a red band around her wrist. He'd always prided himself on his control, on his ability to keep a tight rein on his emotions no matter how provocative the situation. Yet where Lucky was concerned, restraint seemed a thing of the past. She slipped inside his defenses with the agility of a master pickpocket fingering an easy mark. The realization was baffling, and more than a little disconcerting.

Lucky perched on the edge of her desk and resisted the urge to rub her arm. "Just what was it that you wanted to see me about?"

"There's the small matter of a spring carnival," Sam ground out, the words slow and emphatic.

"Yes?"

"An ad in today's paper says you're planning on holding one."

"That's right. Is something wrong with that?"

"Something?" Sam roared incredulously. "Everything's wrong with that!"

Stalling deliberately, Lucky drew a deep breath and ignored the impulse to bolt behind her desk. She hadn't seen Sam this angry since the day he'd first confronted her about her new commercials. Then she'd been prepared. Now she hadn't had the slightest inkling that the plans to host the carnival would prompt this sort of a reaction.

Bracing her hands against the desktop, Lucky faced him with a flat stare and said simply, "Why?"

"For starters, something that size will turn the entire block into a three-ring circus."

"Not a circus," Lucky corrected patiently. "A carnival."

Was she being deliberately obtuse? Sam wondered. Or was it possible that she really didn't understand? "Circus, carnival, what's the difference? However you look at it, the whole idea lacks dignity. It presents the wrong image—"

"For you, maybe." Lucky permitted herself a small smile. Now she was beginning to see what the problem was. But just because she understood didn't mean she agreed. "My customers love it."

Sam muttered an oath under his breath. This was the down side to the unpredictable impetuous streak he'd so admired in Lucky last weekend. He'd suspected all along that one could only throw fate to the wind for so long before the wind turned around and blew it right back. Obviously the time for reckoning had come.

He should have gotten involved with an accountant. Or maybe a nice, tame librarian. Anyone but a tawny-eyed blonde with a penchant for chaos and a marked ability to make his blood pressure rise.

"You can't have thought this all the way through," Sam said firmly. "Where will you find the room to hold something that size?"

"Don't worry about that. Thanks to the commercials, my inventory's way down. The day before the carnival, I'll just move all my stock to the back of the lot so they can set up the rides and booths up front."

"You'll still have people wandering everywhere. Even if you put the cars away, you're bound to find kids sitting on the hoods eating cotton candy, or teenagers climbing in to have a closer look."

"I don't mind." Lucky walked around her desk and sat down. She occupied her hands by straightening her blotter, then aligning her pens in a row beside it. "The cars are

there to be seen, after all. I'm sure a little dirt and a few fin-
gerprints won't ruin them."

Sam suppressed a small shudder at the thought of his
glossy automobiles being subjected to such casual abuse.
He couldn't imagine how she could allow such a thing to
happen, and not only allow it, but genuinely seem not to
care. Though he was beginning to suspect he was fighting
a losing battle, sheer stubbornness wouldn't let him give up
just yet. "What about parking? What are you planning to
do about that?"

Lucky considered for a moment, reaching up with one
hand to rake the curls back off her forehead. Sam had
rapped out the question with all the finesse of a district
attorney cross-examining a reluctant witness. She wasn't
guilty of anything, however, and she was damned if she'd
give him the satisfaction of acting as though she was.

"It'll have to be on the street, I guess. Not perfect, but the
best we can do under the circumstances. Last year, of
course, your lot was empty and everyone parked there, but
now—"

"Last year? You mean you've done this before?"

"Sure, four times. So far, it's always been a huge success."

"I'm sure it has," Sam muttered irritably, finally beginning to accept that even the most logical and eloquent of
arguments weren't likely to alter the situation. Lucky was
enmeshed in another of her harebrained schemes, and unless he missed his guess, he would be going along for the
ride. As he turned to leave, he couldn't resist firing one
parting shot. "I guess some people will do anything for a
little free publicity."

Lucky went absolutely still. "What did you say?"

"You heard me." Sam paused in the doorway and looked
back. "Just do me a favor—if your next stunt involves any

kind of wildlife, say Loonie Louie's pig or maybe a herd of wild buffalo, just give me a few day's notice, okay?"

"Stunt?" Lucky echoed incredulously. "Is that what you think this is—some kind of new promotion to draw in more customers?"

"Isn't it?"

Angry as she was, Lucky found she still couldn't help but appreciate the way Sam's long, lean body filled the doorway, brushed in silhouette by the afternoon sun. She raised her eyes to focus on his face. "I'll have you know this carnival is anything but a publicity stunt. The proceeds go toward a very worthy cause."

"What? The Lucky Vanderholden fund for used-car rehabilitation?"

"No," Lucky said through gritted teeth. "The Better Chance Program of Cloverdale."

"Sounds perfect," Sam said smugly. "Have anything to do with helping old cars reach their full potential?"

"Not cars, Sam, children." Lucky watched with pleasure as her words wiped the satisfied look off his face.

Abruptly he straightened. "What children?"

"Oh you know." Lucky's tone was deliberately offhand. "Underprivileged kids from inner city Philadelphia. The program tries to get them out of the city for the summer— find homes with families in the suburbs or pay their tuition at camp."

Sam swallowed heavily. "*That's* what this spring carnival of yours is all about?"

Lucky nodded.

"Why didn't you say so?"

She sent him a baleful stare. "Did you ever give me a chance?"

He returned the look full measure. "When did you ever wait to be asked?"

"All right, maybe I should have said something, but I just assumed you knew. After all, the carnival's been a spring fixture for years."

"I only moved in last winter," Sam reminded her.

"Besides, I'm sure the ad mentioned the Better Chance program."

It certainly could have, Sam realized. Once he'd seen Lucky's name and address printed at the bottom, he'd been blind to everything else.

"Now would you like to take back all those ridiculous things you said?"

Sam didn't even have to think about that. "Not a chance. The fact still remains that I don't think you have the space to hold something that size on this lot."

"It's worked in the past."

"Donahue Motors wasn't there then. Now it is."

"Too bad you put up that fence . . ." Lucky mused aloud.

"Lucky," Sam intoned, "don't even think about it!"

"All right, I won't touch your precious fence."

"What about insurance?" Sam asked suddenly.

"We're covered."

"Extra lighting in case this thing is still going after dark?"

Lucky didn't have the heart to tell him that last year's carnival had ended well after midnight. "Already arranged."

"Security?"

"Hired. Really, Sam—" Lucky made no attempt to hide her exasperation. "I know what I'm doing. Trust me."

"That's what the captain of the Titanic said."

"Bully for him," Lucky snapped, beginning to grow irritated. Sam had no right to treat her like a wayward child whose actions had to be monitored in order to avoid disaster. She'd survived the first thirty years of her life quite nicely without his interference and, with any luck, she'd manage the next thirty as well.

Deliberately, Lucky opened a drawer and pulled out a ledger. "If you don't mind," she said pointedly, "I'd like to get back to work."

"By all means." Sam waved a hand dismissively. Obviously it didn't bother her at all that she'd ruined his day. He'd be damned if she'd see that it bothered him. "I'd hate to keep you from something important." He continued to talk as he turned and began to walk away. In the stillness of the hot summer afternoon, his voice carried clearly. "I'm sure there must be another holiday coming up that we can arrange a celebration for. Too bad we missed St. Patrick's Day. We could have painted all the cars green . . ."

Too bad indeed, Lucky thought with a grin. Wait until he saw what she had in mind for the Fourth of July.

LUCKY HAD BEEN TELLING the truth when she'd said she had everything under control, but that didn't mean there weren't plenty of details that still had to be attended to. The next morning she took advantage of a lull to leave Clem in charge and drive over to the Better Chance headquarters. She found a parking place in front of the building and was walking up the low flight of steps when the door opened above her and Sam emerged.

Automatically Lucky's gaze skimmed over him. As always he looked devastatingly handsome. Sunlight glinted off the burnished bronze of his hair and warmed the amber tone of his skin. His double-breasted suit was elegant, yet at the same time supremely masculine. Its accent piece was a silk tie with a muted stripe that matched the cool silver gray of his eyes. Yup, thought Lucky as her heart gave a little leap, nothing had changed.

Then she looked up at the building behind him and frowned. What were the chances that Sam's presence there was entirely innocent? To Lucky's dismay, she quickly realized that they weren't nearly as great as the possibility that his visit was somehow connected to the upcoming carnival. She'd paid little heed to his complaints the day before. Perhaps he'd chosen to take them to a higher authority.

Without preamble, Lucky blurted out what was on her mind. "What are *you* doing here?"

"Just leaving," Sam replied, smiling. It was nice to have Lucky be the one who was off balance for a change. He held the door, but still she hesitated on the step. "Are you going in?"

"In a minute." She took the door from him and let it swing shut, then turned and looked at him suspiciously. "Were you talking to the Better Chance people?"

"Actually I was. They're a very nice group—told me all about their program. It seems to be a very worthy cause."

"Then why are you still trying to make things difficult for the carnival?"

"Me?"

"Yes, you! The same man who swept into my office yesterday and all but yelled the walls down."

"I'll admit I may have acted a bit precipitously—"

"A bit?" Lucky hooted.

Sam ignored the interruption. "But that was before I had all the facts. Now that I do, things have changed."

"You mean you think the carnival's a good idea?"

Sam slanted her a look. "Of course not. The way things are arranged, I wouldn't be surprised if you make a shambles of the whole block."

"Then you did come down here to complain."

"No, actually I came down to offer my support."

Lucky hid her surprise with a quick retort. "If you ask very nicely, I bet they'll let you man the dunking booth."

"Thanks, I'll keep that in mind. But I was thinking along the lines of something more practical."

"You're going to open up your lot for parking?" Lucky guessed hopefully, but Sam shook his head.

"If you'd given me more notice, that might have been possible, but as it is, my inventory's too high and I simply haven't got room," Sam said with carefully concealed relief.

"Then what *are* you going to do?"

"Donahue Motors has donated a car."

"A car?" Lucky echoed hollowly.

"To be raffled off."

"One of *your* cars?"

Sam looked at her kindly, as one might regard a backward child. "Who else's?"

"You're giving away a Mercedes?"

"A BMW. Unfortunately it's a little late to publicize the raffle properly, but the people I spoke to inside are convinced they'll still be able to move a lot of tickets."

"I should think so." Lucky whistled softly under her breath. "That's a very generous gesture."

"It's for a good cause. Besides, with the carnival going on right next door, Donahue Motors could hardly remain uninvolved."

"I see what you mean," Lucky said dryly. "It wouldn't have been very good for your image if it looked like you didn't want to participate."

"True." Sam had no intention of rising to the bait Lucky had deliberately tossed his way. "Nevertheless we were happy to help out."

"Anything for a little free publicity?" Lucky smirked, echoing his words from the day before.

"When there's a twenty-five-thousand dollar car on the line, I'd hardly call the benefits free."

"Of course. Heaven forbid we forget the bottom line."

Sam studied Lucky's face intently. "You're determined to goad me today. Why?"

The question brought her up short. Sparring with Sam had been an automatic reflex, a defense against the knife-edged tension that seemed to fill the air whenever they were together. It was either fight with Sam or... No, Lucky decided, quashing the image firmly. She wasn't going to think about that right now.

She glanced upward and saw the uncertainty in Sam's eyes. A second look read concern. He'd always been honest with her, Lucky realized. And he deserved no less in return.

"Maybe you make me nervous," she ventured softly.

"You, nervous?" Sam almost laughed until he saw the expression on her face. Damn if she wasn't serious! "I didn't think anything could rattle a woman who grew up with four brothers."

Lucky's smile was instinctive and purely feminine. "If you imagine for even one moment that I think of you as another brother, then I must have been sending out all the wrong signals."

Sam swallowed a sudden, unexpected breath. It landed in his solar plexus with a jolt. "No," he said slowly, "Not at all."

"Good." Lucky's fingers doodled a soft tattoo on his arm. "Then again," she said thoughtfully, "maybe I make you just the tiniest bit nervous, too."

It was as much a question as a statement. Sam had no intention of admitting how close her suspicions were to the mark. Instead he skirted the issue entirely.

"If that's the case, maybe we should confront our fears together. What are you doing Saturday?"

"Working."

"After that?"

Lucky waggled her eyebrows outrageously. "I'm open to suggestions."

"No prior commitments to Vanderholdens of any size, shape or color?"

"None that I know of."

"That sounds reassuring."

"Sam," Lucky said reproachfully. "You know how my family is."

"I do. That's what scares me." Sam reached around and pulled the door open for her. "I'll pick you up after work. Bring something casual to change into."

"How casual?" Lucky asked as he ushered her inside. "What are we going to do?"

"Oh, I don't know." Sam grinned with devastating effect. "If I were you, I'd be ready for anything."

# 8

A PROMISE LIKE THAT was just the sort of thing that could keep a woman up nights. And it did. Nor, as Lucky realized Saturday morning, was it easy to prepare for. Finally she gave up and called to ask Sam exactly what he had in mind.

"How do you feel about exercise?" he asked.

"Fine, as long as somebody else is doing it."

"Nonsense. You didn't get that body by sitting around on your butt eating bon-bons. How about coming to my club for a workout, then after that we'll grab some dinner?"

Lucky's cheeks warmed with pleasure at the compliment he'd tossed out so casually.

"Bring a leotard," Sam continued, his voice growing low and intimate. "Something sexy and French cut. I'll bet you have beautiful thighs—"

"Sam!"

He chuckled into the phone, and the sound was warm and husky. It washed over Lucky like an incoming tide. "I guess I'll just have to wait and see for myself."

Good Lord, she thought. She was actually blushing. Standing all alone in the middle of her bedroom, wearing nothing but her underwear and turning pink all over. The things that man did to her ought to be outlawed! Either that, she thought with a sigh, or patented.

"Lucky? Still there?"

"Mmm."

"My sentiments exactly," Sam murmured. "See you at six."

The next problem to be solved was that Lucky didn't *have* a French cut leotard. Or, when it came right down to it, any leotards at all. A quick trip into town during her lunch hour remedied that particular dilemma, and Lucky was delighted with her find—a metallic bronze two-piece exercise suit that was outrageously flattering to her slender curves.

Returning to her office, she stuffed the leotard in her duffel bag and didn't give it another thought until almost six. As she was closing up for the night, Lucky saw Sam emerge from the building next door. She waved, then ducked back inside her office to gather up her things. When he drove up, she was waiting.

He smiled with satisfaction as she opened the car door and climbed in. "Finally the weekend begins."

"Speak for yourself. I have to work tomorrow."

"On Sunday?"

"I don't have your kind of support staff," Lucky said without rancor. "Weekends are when I make most of my sales. I missed last Sunday. I don't dare take off another."

Sam frowned. "Would you rather..." He paused. It was an effort to push the words out. "Maybe you'd rather make it another night?"

"Not a chance," Lucky said firmly.

"I'll make sure it's an early evening then."

Her grin flashed like quicksilver. "You can try. As to whether or not you'll succeed..."

Sam glanced over and found himself grinning along with her. On that upbeat note, the evening began. When they reached the health club, Sam escorted Lucky to the ladies' locker room, then continued down the hall to the men's.

She paused a moment at the door, watching him walk away. Even in a suit, his physique was impressive enough to have her libido doing cartwheels. She didn't even want to think about what was going to happen when he emerged wearing considerably less.

Ducking inside, Lucky quickly shed her work clothes and donned the new exercise suit. In the relentless view afforded by the wall-to-wall mirrors, it seemed to cover less than it had in the dressing room that afternoon. Surreptitiously, Lucky cast a glance around. Women of all shapes and sizes paraded around the room in various states of undress. Nobody else seemed self-conscious about the amount of skin they were exposing.

Of course she probably wouldn't be, either, if she didn't have to march outside and face Sam. The skimpy outfit she was wearing left almost nothing to the imagination. All at once Lucky realized that she cared desperately about what Sam might say. Would he find her body attractive? Or would he think she had too much in some places and not enough in others—

"You Lucky?"

She started and spun around. A well-built brunette in a leotard and matching headband was appraising her critically. "Yes, I am."

"There's a man outside waiting for you. Asked me to check and make sure you didn't get lost."

"Oh, thanks."

The brunette watched Lucky gather up her things and shove them into the locker. "Must be your first time."

"How can you tell?"

"Around here, you don't keep any man waiting, much less one that looks like that."

Lucky couldn't help smiling. "I never worry about Sam," she tossed out casually, walking away. "He can take care of himself."

She pushed open the locker room door and immediately saw Sam, leaning against the opposite wall. In the space of a second, her gaze dipped then rose in a lightning-fast appraisal. Abruptly she sucked in a deep, unexpected breath. He looked gorgeous—even better than she'd expected.

Even standing still, Sam exuded a sense of vitality. His body was lean, but hard, and the outfit he wore showed it off to perfection. His T-shirt was old and faded, with the word Stanford stenciled across the front. It clung to Sam like an old friend, delineating the smooth muscles of his chest and the tight line of his waist. His running shorts were of similar vintage and rode low on his lean hips. They covered everything this side of decency, but just barely. His legs were dusted with a sprinkling of dark hairs, the thighs firm and molded, the calves trim.

Even his feet were well shaped, Lucky realized, then gave herself a mental shake. When she started noticing a man's feet, that had to be a sure sign of trouble.

"There you are," Sam said, straightening.

"Sorry I kept you waiting."

"Don't worry." His smoke gray eyes widened appreciatively. "It was well worth it."

To her dismay, Lucky felt herself going warm all over at the insinuation in Sam's tone. She wouldn't blush again, she vowed. She absolutely refused!

"Don't be so sure. Health clubs aren't exactly my usual milieu. I may turn out to be a total flop."

"I doubt it."

Sam cocked his head to one side, studying her with indulgent humor. Then suddenly his hand was sliding around the back of her head to hold her steady as his lips founds hers for a quick, hard kiss. When he straightened, he looked very pleased. "In the past, I've found you to be challenging, exasperating, and at times even infuriating, but never once,

Lucky-love—" Sam paused, lingering over the endearment "—have you been a disappointment. Somehow, I don't think you'll start now."

Breathless, mouth slightly agape, Lucky could only stand and stare as he started toward the Nautilus room.

"Coming?" Sam called back over his shoulder.

"Coming." On feet as light as butterfly wings, she hurried down the hall to catch up.

FORTY-FIVE MINUTES LATER, Lucky knew with certainty how Sam had gotten into such good shape. While she'd initially been intimidated by the gleaming display of Nautilus equipment, he'd moved among the machines like an old pro. He walked her through the program slowly, demonstrating the function of each machine before setting the weights at the lowest level so that she could take a turn.

Much as Lucky tried to force herself to concentrate on the equipment, however, she could not help but be aware of Sam's presence as they worked their way around the room. Repeatedly she was struck by his strength and coordination, so casually displayed as he pitted himself against the finely tuned machines. It was, Lucky discovered, one thing to admire the sculpted perfection of his body standing still, quite another to appreciate its beauty in motion.

By the time they reached the last station in the circuit, Lucky felt pleasantly winded. As always, Sam had let her go first, and now as he adjusted the machine to accommodate his greater strength, she stepped back to simply watch and enjoy.

He sat down and grasped the weighted bar in both hands, steeling himself for the final test. Corded ropes of sinew stood out along the length of his arms. The muscles of Sam's chest tightened and flexed. As the bar began to move in the last series of repetitions, beads of moisture stood out along the sides of his cheeks. Hypnotized, Lucky followed their descent as they skimmed down the strong column of his neck and were absorbed by the soft fabric of his T-shirt.

A dark arrow of sweat stained the front of the T-shirt, and the cotton adhered to Sam's body like a second skin. Lucky's gaze traced the line downward until it disappeared into the waistband of his shorts. Unwittingly her tongue flicked out to moisten her dry lips. Never in her whole life had she been so intensely, so physically aware of a man. Her fingers ached to smooth the damp hair back from his brow. Her lips longed to feel the warm imprint of his. She wanted—

"All done." Sam set the bar carefully aside and rose. "Great workout."

"Mmm-hmm," Lucky agreed weakly. She felt limp and boneless as a wet washcloth. "Great."

"Ready to hit the showers?"

A long cold shower. That was just what she needed to restore her equilibrium. "Sure. I'm all set."

"Good."

Sam's expression was partway between a sigh and a scowl as he followed Lucky back to the locker rooms. It was his own fault, he told himself grimly, his gaze lingering on the pert sway of her cute tush. He'd told Lucky to wear something sexy, and now he could hardly claim innocence when she'd all but knocked his socks off.

Did she have any idea how difficult it had been for him to concentrate on their exercise routine? he wondered. Did she realize there'd been times, watching her muscles strain and her lithe body flex, when he'd wanted nothing more than to cast away the cold steel equipment between them, sweep her up in his arms, and carry her off to someplace dark and quiet?

He'd never thought of working out as a particularly erotic pastime before. But with Lucky beside him, her body enticingly displayed by the clinging leotard, Sam had found his thoughts ranging from mildly lascivious to downright explosive. It had taken every ounce of willpower he possessed to curb his impatience long enough for them to finish the routine.

Now finally it was behind them. Soon he'd have Lucky all to himself. It couldn't happen soon enough.

Lucky quickly showered and dressed. Bypassing the crowds of women waiting to use the makeup mirrors and blow dryers, she styled her hair with her fingers and applied a light coating of gloss to her lips. Even so, Sam was already waiting when she emerged.

"You were quick," she commented as they headed for the exit.

"You'd be amazed how little incentive there is to spend time in a room full of naked men when there's a beautiful woman waiting for you down the hall."

Lucky ducked her head, hiding a smile. Maybe she wasn't the only one who'd been having trouble keeping her mind on the machines. "Where to now?"

Sam pushed open the door and held it as Lucky walked through. "How does Chinese food sound?"

"Perfect."

The restaurant Sam chose was small and unpretentious, a tiny storefront on the main street of a neighboring town. The enthusiasm of its patrons, however, belied the plainness of its exterior. A line had formed in the vestibule that reached out the door and partway down the block. Driving past, Sam parked around the corner and led Lucky to a side door which led directly into the kitchen.

"Ah, Mr. Sam!" A Chinese man looked up from a large hot stove where he was overseeing the preparation of stir-fry vegetables. "So nice to see you again."

"Good evening, Mr. Kwan." The two men were exchanging bows when the swinging door that led to the dining room flew open. Another man, identical to the first except for the sheaf of menus in his hand, came bustling through.

"Mr. Sam and lovely lady," said the new arrival. He grinned and bowed as well. "Your table is all ready."

"Twins?" Lucky asked under her breath as she and Sam followed the second Mr. Kwan out into the dining room.

"Triplets," Sam replied in the same undertone. "The third Mr. Kwan does the books."

"How do you tell them apart?"

"I don't."

Mr. Kwan seated them and took their order for drinks. When he had left, Lucky glanced over to the lobby where the long line was very much in evidence. "Don't you feel guilty jumping ahead of everybody?"

"We didn't jump ahead. I called earlier and made a reservation. Coming in through the kitchen was expedient, that's all."

A moment later, Mr. Kwan served the drinks. Though he was holding menus, he didn't offer them. "Mr. Sam special friend," he announced. "I choose everything. Don't worry, you like."

"I can't wait," Lucky said eagerly. "I'm sure everything will be delicious."

When he'd left once more, Lucky picked up her purse and pulled out a small white envelope. "I have something for you."

"What is it?"

"Open it and see."

Sam lifted the flap and found a pair of pictures, both obviously taken the night of Hal's barbecue. The first was the one they had posed for. Sam's arm was wrapped around

Lucky's waist, his fingers drumming over her ribs. Lucky was looking up and laughing, her eyes startled and filled with delight.

The second picture, however, was entirely different. At some point in the evening, Janice had caught them unaware. They were standing alone, off to one side. Lucky's head was resting on Sam's shoulder; his hand was stroking her hair. There was a soft, almost dreamy quality to the photograph, a look of peacefulness and utter contentment.

Lucky remembered how surprised she'd been when Janice had first shown her the prints. "We don't look like this," she'd declared firmly, tossing the second picture aside. "We fight all the time."

"Tell it to the marines," Janice had retorted. She'd slipped the pictures into an envelope and labeled it with Sam's name. "Now be sure you deliver them *both*. A man with no pictures in his apartment needs all the help he can get. Oh, and Lucky?" she'd added as her sister dropped the parcel in her purse. "Don't forget to tell him that I do enlargements, and I can get a great price on frames."

At the time, Lucky'd been sure that Sam would be interested in neither offer, but now as she watched him lay both prints carefully on the table she realized she was about to be surprised again.

"Wonderful," he said softly, feeling unexpectedly touched by the simple gift.

"Which one?"

"Both." His finger stroked the side of the second print absently. Lucky wondered if he realized he was smiling. "Does your sister have the negatives?"

Lucky nodded. "She said she'd be happy to blow them up if you like."

"Great." Sam gestured toward the first shot. "That one will be perfect for my desk at work. That way, every time I find myself embroiled in another of your schemes, I'll have something to remind me of the few times I've gotten the better of you."

Lucky laughed along with him. "What about the other?"

"That one goes in my bedroom. Right beside my bed."

At his words, Lucky felt a languid sensation of warmth steal over her. It was as though she was floating, cosseted and serene, in a place where everything was wonderful and nothing could possibly go wrong. The euphoric mood remained as the food was served, eaten, then cleared away. Later, Lucky couldn't remember a single thing she'd had. All she knew was that everything had been perfect.

When they both declined dessert, Mr. Kwan brought them a plate that held two fortune cookies, then left them to linger over their wine. Immediately Lucky reached out to pick up the cookie nearest her.

"I always get some silly proverb, but I can never resist looking, anyway," she confessed as she broke open the crisp biscuit and pulled out the strip of white paper. "'You will make a name for yourself,'" she read, then frowned. "I wonder if that's good or bad."

"Good, of course. It means you'll be famous."

"Jesse James was famous. So is Richard Nixon. Sometimes fame isn't all it's cracked up to be."

"In your case, I'm sure you have nothing to fear."

"Oh no? What if I decide to follow Loonie Louie's example—"

"Don't you dare!" Sam broke in with a chuckle. "The day I look out and see a giant pig parading around your lot, you're in big trouble."

Lucky's brow lifted. "Says who?"

Recognizing a loaded question when he heard one, Sam declined to answer. Instead he picked up his wine and gazed at the glass absently. It seemed like a perfect time to change the subject.

"Speaking of names," he commented, "I've been wondering about yours. Having met the rest of your family, I realize that all of them have perfectly normal names, whereas Lucky. . ."

"Is a bit odd," Lucky finished for him with a sigh. "I know."

"Surely you weren't christened that way?"

"Of course not."

"Well?"

"It has to do with first initials," Lucky explained, sampling a piece of her cookie. "One day when we were little, somebody—Frank, I think—realized that if you put everyone else's names in order, they followed the sequence of the alphabet. Emma, Frank, Geoff, Hal, Isabel, Janice, Ken and Marete. See? Every letter but 'L' is accounted for. And there I was, the only one with a name that didn't fit."

"That's when my father said, I don't care if your name isn't right, I still think we're lucky to have you. Of course, in a family like mine, somebody was bound to pounce on that. I've been called Lucky ever since."

Sam reached across the table. His large hand closed over hers, his fingers warm as he squeezed gently. "I think I'm lucky to have you, too."

Lucky smiled, awash with pleasure. She knew she was falling, ever more deeply, for Sam's irresistible allure, but she also knew that she wouldn't have held back for a moment, even if she could. Though their only point of contact was their hands, Lucky felt as though her entire body had been charged with current. Her nerve endings tingled; her face glowed. She felt light and irrepressibly happy.

Her fingers nudged the plate across the table toward Sam. "You haven't looked at your fortune yet."

With his free hand, he took the cookie and cracked it open. He read the message in silence. A long moment passed before he repeated it aloud. "All good things come to those who wait."

"That's not a fortune, it's a proverb."

"Maybe," Sam said softly. "Maybe not."

His gaze found hers, and suddenly the mood shifted, the moment taking on a new and richer texture. Sam's eyes were dark with intent, and Lucky felt the power of his desire tugging within her core.

His voice, when he spoke, was low and husky. "I'm not usually a patient man, Lucky. And it feels as though I've been waiting forever for you...."

Lucky's breath caught in her throat. She started to speak, then stopped, hypnotized by the wealth of sensation that suddenly flooded through her. Only one thought remained clear. She wanted Sam more than she had ever wanted anything in her life.

"Sam?"

His eyes glittered like polished agate in the dim light. "Hmm?"

"Take me home."

## 9

"MY PLEASURE."

Fluidly Sam rose from his chair. As if by magic, the check appeared and was quickly dispatched by his signature at the bottom. As they made their way out onto the sidewalk, the entire evening seemed surrounded by an aura of enchantment, blessed by a bewitching blend of mystery and expectation that could only auger well for what was to come.

They climbed into the BMW and the engine started with its customary purr. As the car pulled away from the curb, Lucky leaned her head back against the seat, savoring the delicious feeling of anticipation that hummed in her veins. Right at that moment, she was the luckiest woman alive.

Which is why it came as such a shock ten minutes later when the car broke down.

The first sign of trouble was a seize and a sputter in the engine; the second, a loss of power on a mild hill. From there, things grew steadily worse. "Can we make it back to Cloverdale?" Lucky asked, sitting up.

"I don't think so." Sam nursed the ailing car another quarter mile before it stalled. He switched on his flashers and guided it to the shoulder of the dark, deserted road. "Damn!"

Lucky swiveled around to look in both directions. No lights were visible either way. Beside her Sam was fishing around beneath the driver's seat. After a moment he came up with a flashlight. "I'm going to get out and have a look."

"I'll help."

Sam glanced at her and nodded. In the dim light, Lucky's eyes were huge and luminous. Her features were drawn with concern, and something else, Sam realized. Frustration?

Involuntarily he reached up to stroke the slope of her cheek. "I'm sorry. I wish like hell this hadn't happened."

"So do I." Lucky smiled, her fingers closing over his. "Let's go look. Maybe it's something we can fix ourselves. And if it doesn't take too long . . ."

Lucky didn't finish the thought. She didn't have to. They both knew what remained unsaid, and what, hopefully, still lay ahead.

Sam pulled the lever that released the hood, then hopped out and braced it up. As Lucky held the flashlight, he began a quick check of the equipment. Peering over his shoulder, Lucky conducted a visual survey of her own. Life with four brothers had provided her with a thorough education where engines were concerned. And the time she'd spent with Sam had provided her with something else—a strong incentive to get the car running again, fast.

The hoses, Lucky could see, were still all in order. Nor was the way the car had stalled indicative of that sort of problem. Absently she watched as Sam checked the distributor cap, then the spark plugs, coming up empty both times.

"The fuel line," she said suddenly.

Sam looked up. "What about it?"

"The way the car sputtered and bucked before it died— I'll bet anything you got a tank of bad gas and there's dirt in your lines. Here, hold this a minute, would you?" Without thinking, Lucky passed the flashlight over to Sam and assumed control.

Bending over the engine, she unsnapped the air filter and lifted it free. "There." She pointed with her finger to direct the beam. "Your gas filter—see, it's all clogged."

"Of course," Sam agreed hollowly, as he went around to the trunk for the tool chest.

Too pleased by her discovery to notice his lack of enthusiasm, Lucky dug around in the chest until she found what she needed. As Sam aimed the light, she quickly set about rectifying the problem.

Damn it, thought Sam. He ought to be thrilled that their dilemma was nothing serious. Barring that, he should, at the very least, be admiring Lucky's calm, capable handling of the situation. But to tell the truth, neither emotion came close to expressing the way he felt.

Sam pointed the light as he'd been told and frowned grimly. Superfluous—that was the way he felt. And he didn't like it one bit.

He was used to taking care of himself, to being independent and in control, and he ceded neither right easily. Lucky, however, had never stopped to consider how he might feel. In her usual headstrong fashion she'd simply plunged right in and gone to work, leaving nothing for him to do but stand around like a dime-store dummy holding on to the damn flashlight.

Watching as she worked, Sam tried in vain to recapture the tenderly romantic mood they'd enjoyed throughout most of the evening. It just wouldn't wash. Lucky had steamrolled right through his emotions, shunting aside protective and amorous impulses alike, leaving nothing in their wake save a grudging respect for her mechanical skills.

Unfortunately, Sam thought with a scowl, that was not the sort of thing that would tempt a man to take a woman to his bed.

"All set," Lucky announced. "Why don't you get in and give it a try?"

Sam did, and the car started immediately.

Lucky put the tools away and climbed in beside him. "There's probably more dirt in those lines. I only got what was in the filter. You ought to get one of your mechanics to look at it tomorrow."

"Thanks," said Sam, his voice clipped. "I will."

Lucky tossed a glare in his direction and slammed her door with unnecessary force. Only an idiot could have been unaware of the silent air of disapproval with which Sam had watched her make the repair. And only a fool wouldn't realize that the high hopes she'd harbored for the evening's outcome were now nothing short of an impossible dream.

Something had changed during that brief stop by the side of the road, something that went far beyond the inconvenience the breakdown had caused. Before there'd been a reckless, happy feeling of complicity. Now there was only silence. And Lucky hadn't the slightest idea why.

"All right," she said finally. "Out with it."

Sam glanced briefly in her direction, then turned his eyes back to the road. "With what?"

"You've been scowling for the past ten minutes. I want to know why."

"I should think the reason for that was fairly obvious. I've heard it said that timing is everything, but never have I seen the point more vividly illustrated."

Lucky reached over and laid a hand on Sam's arm. "Yes, but we're on our way again now, and it's not *that* late."

"Late enough." Sam knew he was behaving like an idiot, knew and couldn't seem to do a single thing about it. "You told me yourself that you have to be up early."

"Why don't you let me worry about that?"

Sam slanted her a baleful look. "I've seen you in action, Lucky. You don't worry. You just jump right in—damn the torpedoes and full speed ahead."

So that was it. Lucky pulled back her hand, knitting her fingers together in her lap. "You didn't like that I fixed your car."

"I wouldn't say that."

"You don't have to." Lucky sighed softly, wondering what she should have done differently. She'd never modified her behavior for any man, and she was not about to start now. Not even for Sam. "I grew up with a houseful of brothers, okay? Rebuilding old cars was just something to do on a Saturday afternoon. I'm sorry if I stepped on your toes back there, but I saw something that needed fixing, and it never occurred to me not to do it, that's all."

She really meant it, Sam realized. His irritation ebbed, only to be replaced, seconds later, by remorse. It was a sad commentary on the state of his life when a simple offer of aid from a friend could be misconstrued as an attempt at one-upmanship. No wonder Lucky hadn't been concerned about his precious independence, he thought wryly, she'd been too damn busy fixing the car!

"Don't apologize," Sam said gruffly. "I'm the one who should be sorry." He turned the car down her street and coasted to a stop before her house. Flicking off the engine, Sam reached over to slide his hand around her neck, his fingers gliding through her hair. "There's no excuse for the way I acted. All I can say is that I guess I'm just used to being the boss."

Lucky sent him a measuring look. "So am I."

In spite of all that had happened, Sam still found it was an effort not to smile. "You're not going to let me off easy, are you?"

"Never."

"That's what I was afraid of."

"No," Lucky said honestly. "That's what you respect."

"You're right," Sam agreed and drew her toward him, narrowing the gap between them. "I do respect you. If I didn't, we wouldn't be here."

Lucky's gaze dipped downward, focusing on Sam's rounded lower lip. For some reason, she couldn't seem to look away. "Too late to butter me up now, Donahue."

He grinned at her in the half-light, that silly, sexy lopsided grin that made her insides melt. "Are you sure?"

His voice was husky, its tone rife with promise. All at once, a flame of rekindled desire licked along Lucky's nerve endings. Warmth rose to her cheeks as her body began to tingle with anticipation. "I guess that depends."

"On?"

Her gaze lifted to meet Sam's. "On how much energy you're willing to expend changing my mind."

"For you," he promised, "I'm willing to give it everything I've got."

The distance between them faded as Sam reached up to cradle Lucky's face in his palms, holding her steady while his mouth lowered to hers. Gently their lips touched, separated for the space of a heartbeat, then came together again.

Slowly Lucky's eyes slid shut as a spear of sensation shivered through her. When Sam would have drawn back, her hands came up over his chest, tangling in the soft cotton of his shirt and holding him near. The clean male scent of him filled her nostrils. The silken caress of his tongue skimming over her lips made her tremble with need.

Her mouth opened to him and for an endless moment nothing else mattered save the deepening kiss and the pleasure that radiated between them. His tongue found hers and began a seduction all its own. Lucky knew his taste and she savored it, just as she savored the heat that shimmered through her body, through her mind. Willingly she gave herself up to the primitive enjoyment of being in Sam's arms. Wantonly her fingers stumbled over the buttons of his shirt.

When the placket finally came free, she slipped her hands inside the warm material, palms flattened against the hard wall of his chest. The harsh intake of Sam's breath tightened the muscles of his gut as his tongue thrust deep into Lucky's mouth. His hands raked through her hair, then settled on her shoulders. She was still too far away. Impatiently he reached to draw her into his lap only to have his efforts defeated by the cramped confines of the car.

"Damn!" Sam swore vehemently. "This is madness!"

The taste of him still warm on her lips, Lucky slowly opened her eyes. Moonlight washed through the windshield creating a play of light and shadow across the planes of Sam's face. His eyes were hooded, his expression fierce. It might be madness, thought Lucky, but such sweet lunacy made rational thought a poor second.

"Sam—"

He gave a short, violent shake of his head. One more word and he would lose control entirely. "I'd better get you inside while I can still walk."

"But Sam . . ."

Once again he didn't wait to hear what she had to say. Instead he flung open the car door, then flung himself out with equal ferocity. Lucky looked at the rigid set of his shoulders and sighed. He'd said earlier that it was too late. Apparently nothing that had happened since had been enough to change his mind. By the time he opened the passenger door and reached in a hand to draw her out, she'd resigned herself to being escorted to her door.

"I guess I should be touched that you're concerned about the time," she said as they climbed the steps. It wasn't until she'd stopped by the door, key out and reaching for the lock, that she glanced up and saw the incredulous look on Sam's face.

"Time, hell!" he gritted. "I was worried about the gear shift."

"The gear shift?" Lucky echoed uncomprehendingly.

When a moment passed and she hadn't moved, Sam took the key ring from her nerveless fingers and unlocked the door. It swung inward, and a triangle of light pooled at their feet. Still Lucky didn't move. She looked inside, then slowly back at Sam. "You mean you're coming in?"

"Of course, what did you . . ." Sam's voice trailed away as he read the confusion on her face. His hands came up, fingers tensing as they gripped the tops of her arms and turned her gently to him. "That is, I'm coming in if you want me to."

Lucky smiled tremulously in the half light. "I do."

"You're sure?"

Her eyes were dark with passion as she lifted her gaze to his. "Very."

With a strangled groan, Sam reached down and swept Lucky into his arms. Two steps took them into the front hall. Sam paused only long enough to kick the door shut behind them before heading for the stairs.

Lucky turned her face inward, feeling the power of Sam's muscular body, inhaling the tangy musk of his scent. Desire vibrated between them. She felt it in the coiled sinew of Sam's arms, heard it in the uneven cadence of his breath. The hand that cradled her thighs stroked the curve of her hip absently. The caress was as tender as it was erotic, and Lucky trembled beneath his gentle touch.

The first door Sam came to led to Lucky's room. Moonlight spilled in through the lace-curtained windows, creating a gossamer shaft of illumination to light the way. He strode to the bed, then stopped just beside it.

The arm beneath Lucky's shoulders held steady as Sam's other hand released her legs. She pivoted slightly, then let her body slide slowly, sensually, down the length of his. Sam's deep, low groan followed her descent.

He'd never felt like this before, consumed by a desire so fierce that it could drive a man wild. The need that had begun when he'd first kissed Lucky in the car throbbed through every fiber of his being. He'd never swept a woman off her feet before. One small part of his brain refused to believe that he had done it now. All he knew was that he'd had to wrap her in his arms, had to feel the heated friction of her body nestled against his own—had to, or forever rue the loss.

Standing on her toes before him, Lucky reached up and nudged aside the open front of Sam's shirt. Turning her face from side to side, she caressed his chest with her cheeks, her lips, her heated breath. The play of texture fascinated her—the smooth skin, hard muscle and the crisp sprinkling of dark hair that brushed her sensitized skin.

As her fingers found the small bud of his nipple and stroked it to a hard point, Sam felt a shock of sensation ripple through him. His hands dragged her closer. Bending his head, he rained a veil of kisses over the soft skin of Lucky's neck. She gasped, and the sudden intake of breath sent a shiver of pleasure racing across his skin. His palms cupped her face, lifting it to his. His tongue sank deep within her mouth, withdrew, then plunged again.

Lucky's head began to spin as thought whirled away and pleasure became all. An ache was building deep inside her, a feverish, pulsating need that sent her blood pounding in her veins. Straining against him, she nestled in the cradle of Sam's thighs, her body pressed against his rigid manhood. As one they began to move, their bodies perfectly synchronized, the rhythm as old as time.

"Lucky?" Sam asked softly.

"Yes," she murmured, the word whispered on a sigh. "Oh, yes!"

They parted just far enough to pull off their clothing. Eagerly Lucky pushed Sam's shirt from his shoulders. Impatiently her fingers wrestled with his belt buckle, then eased his pants downward. A tiny scrap of blue material low on his hips held the bulging evidence of his manhood.

As she reached to relieve him of this last bit of clothing, Sam laughed softly and caught her hands in his. "My turn," he said.

Grasping the hem of her top, he lifted it up over her shoulders and away. Bathed by the moonlight, Lucky's body gleamed like alabaster. Her breasts, small and high, were encased in lace. Slowly, reverently, Sam unfastened the clasp and eased the edges of her bra aside.

"I knew you'd look like this," he said, his hands cupping the weight of her breasts. "Perfect."

In an automatic response, Lucky shook her head. But when she would have spoken, Sam reached up and covered her lips with one finger. "Perfect," he repeated softly.

She smiled then and said nothing at all, letting the single word hover in the air between them like a talisman as they quickly finished undressing. Side by side they lay down on the bed, their hands reaching, touching, in a frenzy of exploration. Lucky's fingers skated over Sam's rib cage, then traced the hard ridge of muscle across his stomach. Her breath coming in short, hot strokes, she bent to bathe him with lips and tongue.

When she would have dipped lower, Sam's large hands caught her, dragging her back to his side. His mouth crushed down on Lucky's, swallowing her gasp and the tiny, ragged cries that followed it as the easy, languid strokes of his hand sent ripples of intoxicating pleasure radiating through every inch of her being. Tension coiled and grew within her, spiraling outward and drawing her closer to a whirling vortex of mindless sensation.

"I need you so much," she whispered. "I need to feel you inside of me."

"Tell me. Just tell me what you want."

"All of you," Lucky said simply and Sam's breath lodged in his throat.

Reaching behind her, she drew open a drawer in the night table beside the bed and pulled out a small foil packet. Quickly she arranged the sheath that would protect them both.

Watching her through hooded eyes, Sam knew that he was balanced on the ragged edge of control. He'd never known a woman who excited him as Lucky did, nor one he wanted more. No sooner was she finished than he laid her back down upon the mattress.

Lucky's thighs parted, her hands reaching up eagerly to guide him, then there was a rush of pure sensation as he slipped inside and made them one. When he would have paused, giving her time to adjust, her body arched upward, driving him ever deeper into her sweet, wet heat.

Reeling with pleasure, Lucky gathered him to her. She hadn't known it was possible to feel like this, full and at the same time, fulfilled, as though time and place had no meaning, as though nothing mattered at all save the ecstasy that built and swirled within her. "Sam . . . !"

He heard her whisper his name, the sound part incantation, part plea. Her hips undulated beneath him, chasing his movement, catching it; starting, stopping and driving him mad. Her head whipped back and forth across the pillow and his fingers plunged into her hair as he covered her mouth with his own.

Awed by his power, by the ferocity of the sensations that rocketed through her, Lucky tried to speak but could only gasp as pleasure broke and splintered through her like heat lightning in a summer sky. Soft rippling waves of incandescent sensation drew Sam deeper, ever deeper, until he could hold on no longer. Ecstasy burst upon him as, with a hoarse cry, he lost himself in his own release.

Long moments passed before either one spoke, their labored breathing the only sound in the shadow-lit room. Tenderly Sam gazed down upon her. Gently his fingers smoothed the tangled curls from her damp brow. Though her eyes were closed, her expression was one of pure satisfaction.

Smiling, Sam brushed a kiss across her lips. "You look very pleased with yourself."

"Actually," Lucky murmured, opening one eye. "I'm very pleased with you."

He lifted himself slightly away, bracing his weight on his elbows. "Under the circumstances, I'll take that as a compliment."

"Under the circumstances, you may take it as a ringing endorsement."

"Ringing?"

"I heard bells." Lucky cocked a brow innocently. "Didn't you?"

"Was that what they were?"

Feeling inordinately smug, Lucky nodded. "Next time you'll have to listen more carefully."

"Next time?"

She arched beneath him, her hips lifting to meet his. "Umm-hmm."

"Oh." Sam grinned wolfishly.

"Oh, indeed."

This time they both heard them.

# 10

THE FOLLOWING SUNDAY the carnival went off without a hitch.

In the intervening week, Sam had made a conscious effort to remain in the background. He knew Lucky was busy, and he found himself unwilling to offer too much assistance, lest his involvement be seen as interference. Still, they spoke on the phone often, and Sam watched with growing pride as Lucky whipped all the diverse elements of the affair into shape. By the time Sunday arrived, not a single thing of major proportion had gone wrong. As for the minor crises, she simply took them as they came, solving each with the same calm efficiency that marked her approach to life in general.

A last-minute advertising blitz had drawn statewide attention to the raffle, and requests for tickets poured in. Like the star it was, the BMW spent all day Sunday featured prominently in the middle of the midway. At Sam's suggestion, it was cordoned off from prying hands and sticky fingers by a rolled, blue velvet rope. Even so, a crowd gathered to ogle the car appreciatively, and the ticket booth that had been set up beside it did a brisk business.

By the time the winning number was drawn, with great fanfare, at eight o'clock that night, thousands of dollars had been made and the anticipation had reached fever pitch. A loud shriek announced the winning ticket holder, a school teacher from Cloverdale Elementary, who stepped up onto the stage to claim the key to the ignition from Sam.

Immediately reporters from the local press gathered around. When they'd finished snapping pictures of the teary-eyed winner, they descended upon Sam, who was standing at the edge of the stage with Lucky. "Mr. Donahue? Could we have a word?"

"Sure," said Sam, smiling expansively. When Lucky tried to step back into the crowd, he took her hand and held on tightly.

"Is it true that all the proceeds from the raffle are being donated to the Better Chance Program?"

"Yes, it is."

"That must be quite a sum."

"We don't have the final figures yet..." Sam tugged Lucky forward into the light. "And of course that amount would be only a part of the total achieved by the carnival itself. This is Lucky Vanderholden whose generous donation of time and facilities were responsible for making the event a reality."

"Speaking of generosity..."

The questions flew at them from all directions. Sam took some, while Lucky fielded others. Through it all she was aware how often Sam turned the subject away from his own contribution, citing others whom he felt deserved credit, or emphasizing the worthiness of the program itself. Far from using the raffle to promote his own image, Sam seemed content instead to downplay his part in the entire affair.

"You know," Lucky said when the reporters had finished and moved on. "You really are a very nice man."

Sam's eyes gleamed with amusement. "Was there ever any doubt?"

"Once or twice—" Sam jabbed her in the ribs and she dodged to one side, laughing. "Make that three times!"

As she spun away, laughing and unutterably lovely, he caught her and pulled her into his arms. A quick glance

around confirmed the inappropriateness of their surroundings. "Lord," he growled softly, "the things you tempt
me to do."

Lucky read the look of dark intent in his eyes. "Don't you
dare," she warned, half-eager, half-amused. "You'll shock
everyone in town."

"I have no intention of kissing you on a well-lit stage."
Sam's arm circled her shoulders, holding her to his side as
he strode toward the steps. "I have a much better idea."

"Where?" Lucky asked breathlessly.

"Ever neck on a Ferris wheel?"

She shook her head.

"Well, you're about to start."

Lucky tried to maintain a look of dignity and decorum
as Sam surreptitiously slipped the ride operator a bill and
gestured toward the top. She was sure that everyone in line
had read his meaning and was frankly too pleased to care.
Then they were climbing in the car and being swept sky-
ward into the star-filled night.

Two spins later the wheel shut down, Lucky and Sam's
car dangling from the top. Grinning, the operator pulled out
some tools and began to fiddle with the controls.

"You're a menace," Lucky said, laughing.

"I know." Sam held out his arms and she flowed into
them, her spirit soaring as high as clouds.

THE FIRST THING Lucky did the next morning when she
reached her office was call Sam. "Hello?" he growled,
sounding more than a little distracted.

"It's me."

Immediately his tone changed. "I was just thinking about
you."

"That sounds promising."

"It was. I was imagining what might have happened if that Ferris wheel operator had managed to stall for just a few more minutes."

"Sam!" Lucky tried to sound shocked; she had to settle for amused. "I never realized you had such exhibitionist tendencies."

"Neither did I." The growl was definitely back.

Lucky stifled a laugh and changed the subject. "Let me tell you why I'm calling. I have a proposition for you."

"Shoot."

"I'd rather talk about it in person. Do you have ten minutes?"

"Sure. I'll be right over."

True to his word, Sam was soon standing in Lucky's doorway. On his way there, he'd admired the speed with which her operation was being returned to normal. Almost all the rides and booths had been dismantled and shipped out the night before, and now a clean-up crew was hard at work sweeping away the last of the debris. The only thing he couldn't understand was a loud, persistent banging that was coming from the direction of the garage.

"Have a seat," Lucky invited, apparently oblivious to the racket.

Sam carefully chose the sturdier of the two chairs. "What's all that noise?"

"I think it's the elephant."

"Of course." Sam's eyes narrowed. "What elephant?"

"The one they were giving rides on last night. Apparently when the carnival was over, he balked at getting into the truck. I gather it's difficult to force an elephant to do something he doesn't want to do. He spent the night in one of the bays."

"I see." Sam leaned back gingerly, having long since accepted that comfort and stability were alien notions where

Lucky's office chairs were concerned. "Speaking of the elephant, somehow you never got around to mentioning him beforehand. Why is that?"

Lucky's expression was carefully deadpan. "I wanted to surprise you."

"I'll bet," Sam muttered. "Just for the record, do you have any other surprises planned?"

"Not really..."

"Hold on to your hats, ladies and gentlemen. Here we go again."

"For pete's sake!" Lucky snapped. "It's only a float."

"As in root beer?"

"Of course not. As in Fourth of July parade."

Sam considered that for a moment, then asked carefully, "Are there any animals involved?"

"Not a one."

He relaxed fractionally and the flimsy wooden chair gave an ominous creak. The small noise was followed by a loud thump that shook the back of the building. Ignoring it, Sam pressed on gamely. "I suppose I could give the idea some thought—"

"There's nothing for you to think about," Lucky broke in. "The float is sponsored by my lot, Donahue Motors doesn't have to be involved at all."

Sam looked up. "I thought you said you had a proposition for me."

"I do." Lucky rose and walked out from behind her desk. "But that's not it."

"Somehow, when you begin to pace, I suspect I'm in trouble."

Lucky shot a glare downward. "I'm not pacing!"

"Not yet," Sam replied calmly.

The elephant trumpeted loudly just outside and the sound raised the hackles on the back of Lucky's neck. Wheeling around, she stuck her head out the open window. "Cut that out," she warned, "or I'll take you home to meet my family!" She watched for another minute, and when she pulled her head back in she was smiling.

"Did it work?"

"Like a charm," Lucky said smugly.

"Why am I not surprised?" Sam inquired of no one in particular.

Lucky gave him a withering look. "Do you want to hear my idea or not?"

Sam folded his hands in his lap and smiled benignly. "I'm ready when you are."

It was, Lucky told herself, a perfectly brilliant idea. So why was she stalling? Ever since Sam's car had broken down, the thought had been percolating in her subconscious. Then this past weekend, when she'd seen how much good they were able to accomplish when they pooled their efforts as they had for the carnival, she'd known that a joint venture was the perfect next step. Now if only Sam would agree.

"I've been thinking that you and I might want to consider going into business together."

Sam's brow rose at that, as she'd figured it might. Quickly Lucky hurried on.

"I know how much you enjoyed that Roll Royce we saw at the auto fair, and it occurred to me that a car like that is the perfect balance between our two sets of objectives. It's old, but at the same time, very beautiful. When you looked at that car, you didn't just appreciate it for what it was, you appreciated it for what it is today, an elegant and valuable piece of machinery."

"True." Though he thought he had a fair idea where she was heading, Sam decided to let Lucky spell things out to him.

"I don't know if you realize it or not, but a lot of people are interested in old cars, and there's a thriving business to be done in restoration."

"Lucky, if I wanted to deal in used cars—"

"Not just any used cars!" she broke in before he could voice his objections. "But classics, one-of-a-kind models, luxury cars that have gone to seed but can still be restored to their former glory. I'm talking about Rolls Royces, Mercedeses, Corvettes—cars whose value hasn't diminished over the years. A model like that, in mint condition, is a find, and they always bring premium prices."

Sam sat for a moment in thoughtful silence. He'd never given the second-hand market a thought; the idea had never interested him in the slightest before. But now, thinking back to that beautiful Rolls, he realized that for an automobile like that, he could be tempted.

"What makes you think we could be successful at it?"

Lucky spun around, her hands gesturing excitedly. "Your mechanics are the experts when it comes to luxury imports. Mine can take any car alive, no matter how old, and make it run. You have access to the parts and special paints we'll need, and I know just about the best body man in the business. How can we miss?"

Sam found himself grinning at the vibrant quality of Lucky's enthusiasm. He was watching a born saleswoman in action—watching and enjoying every minute. "You've obviously given the larger concept some serious thought, but how about the small details?"

"Such as?"

"Record keeping, for one. Decision making, for another. I think we ought to agree up front whether both of us would have to be in on each purchase and sale, or whether we'd be willing to trust each other's judgment."

"That's easy," Lucky replied. "I'm sure I'd be happy with any business decisions you made. Besides, if each of us was empowered to act independently, there'd be less chance of our missing out on something we might really want."

"Agreed."

"As to record keeping, I'm pretty flexible. How would you like to handle it?"

Sam cast Lucky's aging file cabinet a disparaging glance. "At my place."

"Fine." Lucky smiled at the direction of his gaze. "I have no problem with that."

"There is one other thing..."

Lucky waited in silence for him to continue, confident that she hadn't overlooked anything.

"Business almost succeeded in coming between us once before. Have you considered the possibility that it might happen again?"

"I did, but then I also remembered how much fun we had resolving our differences." She paused to waggle her eyebrows wickedly. "On the whole, I decided it was worth the risk."

Sam tried to look stern, but within seconds his grin was every bit as wide as hers. No doubt about it, Lucky's idea had more than enough merit to make him stop and think. His instincts, the ones he was used to trusting implicitly, told him the plan might be worth a try.

"So," he said. "Where do we get the cars?"

"You mean you'll actually do it?"

Sam nodded.

"But..." Lucky sputtered in surprise. "I haven't even used my best arguments yet!"

"Save them. You never know when a good argument will come in handy."

Quickly, before he had a chance to change his mind, Lucky pulled out a piece of paper and roughed out a newspaper ad. "Clem always has his eye out for a bargain, so I wouldn't be surprised if he knows about a car or two," she said as she handed it over. "But in the meantime, what do you think of running this in the *Inquirer*?"

"'Classic cars wanted for restoration,'" Sam read aloud. "'All models, all years considered. Top prices paid.' That should get us some attention all right, especially the part about the top prices. And speaking of which—" he paused and glanced up "—which one of us is contributing the start-up money for this little venture?"

"Both, of course. We'll split the expenses and the profits fifty-fifty." Lucky aimed a smug look in Sam's direction. "The genius on my part, for thinking it up, comes free."

"So that's what it was. I'm glad you told me, I might not have recognized it."

She tilted her nose in the air. "Einstein had his detractors, too."

"Thank goodness he didn't deal in used cars." Sam folded the ad and placed it in his pocket. "If you like, I'll call this in when I get back to my office. We should be able to get ourselves listed by the end of the week."

Lucky watched as he stood up, his long body uncoiling from the small chair. "You're really going to go through with this, aren't you?"

"Of course. I told you. I think it's a good idea."

"I know, but—"

"But what?"

Lucky shrugged. "It's just that I expected you to tell me that you had to think about it, or do some research, or maybe read a bunch of market reports. I certainly hoped you'd agree in the end, but to do it so quickly... well, it just took me by surprise, that's all."

If the truth were told, Sam had taken himself by surprise, too. Where was the innate caution he'd once prided himself upon? The calm deliberation with which he'd always approached new business ventures in the past? Granted, he *had* found the idea more than a little enticing. But even so, jumping in so precipitously just wasn't like him at all. There was only one person he knew who made decisions with that particular brand of impetuousness....

Sam stared at Lucky suspiciously. "This is all your fault."

"I don't doubt it for a minute," Lucky agreed. She waited a moment, but when he declined to enlighten her, she asked, "What is?"

Sam braced his hands on the edge of Lucky's desk, and leaned forward so that he towered over her. "Before I met you, I was a calm, rational person. I looked before I leaped, thought before I talked—"

"And flossed after every meal?"

"This is serious!" Sam growled. "You realize there's only one explanation—some of that impetuous nature of yours is rubbing off on me."

Lucky stifled a laugh. "A fate worse than death, I'm sure."

Sam shook his head irritably. "It should have worked the other way around. Now *that* would make sense!"

"It has worked the other way," Lucky informed him, laughing now in earnest. "Since I met you, I've become much more conservative. Next thing you know, I'll be wearing a paisley bow tie and voting Republican."

Sam's answer to that was an audible snort. Clearly he was not impressed by her supposed transformation. Before he could argue the point, however, they were interrupted by a brawny, bearded man who stuck his head in the open door and asked, "Hey, aren't you supposed to be the lady who sells cars?"

"Yes I am." Immediately Lucky rose to her feet. "I'll be right with you."

"Well before you bother coming out, I think you'd better know, there aren't any cars out here."

For a moment, Lucky could only manage a blank stare. Then suddenly, she remembered. "Right. We had to move them for the carnival. Everything we have is around back. I'll be happy to show you—"

"Take your time." He waved a restraining hand in her direction. "Finish your business, I'll just head out back by myself."

"It's just as well," Sam said as the man disappeared. "I have to be going anyway. Somehow, whenever I'm around you I tend to forget all about other things, like Donahue Motors."

"I'm not sure that's a compliment," Lucky said, considering. "But I guess I can give it the benefit of the doubt."

"Do that."

As Lucky came out from behind her desk, Sam pulled her into his arms. His mouth closed over hers, joining them in a kiss that was brief, but devastating in its intensity. When he set her free, Lucky wobbled on her feet.

"Dinner?" she managed shakily.

"At nine-thirty in the morning?"

She gave him the look the comment deserved.

"I'm afraid I can't." He sounded genuinely sorry. Still, Lucky felt disappointment rocket through her like a blow.

"I have a good friend coming in from out of town. He's only going to be in the area one night, and I promised to keep it free."

"Terrific," said Lucky, her disappointment lifting. "I'd love to meet him."

"You can't be serious. Do you have any idea what old college buddies do when they get together? They sit around, drink beer and talk about the good old days."

"Fine," Lucky replied, undaunted. Having inundated Sam with her relatives, she was delighted by the chance to meet someone that he cared about. "I'll sit around, drink beer and listen."

"If that's what you really want . . ."

"I do." Lucky hooked an arm around his waist as they walked outside to the lot.

"Peter's due to arrive around six. We'll swing by and pick you up."

"Great." Lucky watched as Sam walked away, his long strides making short work of the distance to the road. If it was never going to occur to him to bulldoze that fence, she might be tempted into doing it herself. Then, with a last look, she pulled her gaze reluctantly away and hurried around the back of the building to see if she could make a sale.

THE BURLY MAN with the beard bought an ancient Toyota that Lucky had been trying to unload for months. Though the car was barely large enough to accommodate his bulk, and the engine sounded as though it was being strained to the limit by the effort of conveying him around, he seemed pleased by his choice. Lucky, for her part, was delighted.

Though not superstitious by nature, she had long ago decided that a sale first thing Monday morning augured well for the rest of the week. It seemed clear that she was not going to be disappointed when she made her second sale just that afternoon. Two cars sold in one day was a record for Lucky's Late-Model Lovelies, and she was in high spirits when it was time to close that evening.

The sales had a lot to do with that. But then, of course, there was Sam. Every time she thought about him she felt the most peculiar little flutter in the pit of her stomach. And every time she remembered the heat that washed through her when Sam held her in his arms . . . well!

Much as she enjoyed spending time alone with Sam, Lucky found herself relishing the opportunity that the evening would bring. It would be interesting to watch Sam interact with an old friend. So far, the facets of his personality he'd revealed had covered a broad range. There was the hard driving businessman she'd met first, the slightly aloof gentleman who'd accompanied her to the car fair, and then the incredibly tender lover who had taken her to his bed.

Only recently had Sam begun to relax enough to give free rein to the teasing, more playful side of his personality. And only recently, Lucky mused, had she realized she was falling in love with him.

The knowledge came to her just that quietly, as though it was the most natural, most obvious thing in the world. Then that realization was followed by another, more sobering thought. It was one thing to be sure of her feelings for Sam, and quite another to try and guess what his for her might be. In many ways love was the ultimate risk. Did she dare hope it would be possible to persuade a man who prided himself on his caution to take that chance?

Because she didn't have an answer to the question, Lucky was determined to put it out of her mind. She pulled out the previous month's ledger and was systematically balancing the books when she heard Sam's car pull up outside. Quickly she slammed the ledger shut and hurried out to meet him.

Sam's friend, Peter DiNardo, was not at all what Lucky had expected. Slight of build, with bright red hair and a face covered in freckles, he looked like a young, earnest Jimmy

Olsen. Add that to warm blue eyes and an easy smile and Lucky knew right away that they were going to be friends.

"I'll follow you in my car," she said when the introductions had been completed. "That way, you won't have to bring me back here later."

Within fifteen minutes' time, they were ensconced in Sam's kitchen. True to his word, he'd offered beer all around. No sooner were they settled than the doorbell rang, and Peter jumped up eagerly.

"Are we expecting someone else?" asked Lucky.

Sam unknotted his tie, slid if free of his collar and tossed it on the counter. "Dinner."

"Shame on you. Your best friend comes to town and you *send out*?"

"He didn't." Peter came back carrying two large boxes of fragrant pizza. "I did. What's beer without the proper accompaniment?"

"I succumb to your logic." Lucky inhaled happily, breathing in the rich aroma as Sam flipped open the top of the first box. The pizza, prepared with all the trimmings, looked wonderful. Sam supplied the plates and a stack of napkins and the three of them dug in hungrily.

Predictably, no sooner had the edge been taken off their appetites than the talk turned back to Sam and Peter's college days. Perched on a stool at the end of the counter, Lucky was content to listen to the two men reminisce, laughing along with them as they recounted anecdotes centering on students and teachers alike.

"You'd never know it to look at him now," Peter said, gesturing toward Sam with a wedge of pizza, "but in those days, he had hair down to his shoulders."

"Never," Sam said with dignity.

"All right then, your chin."

Lucky grinned at Sam's sheepish look.

"Maybe," he allowed.

"No maybes about it!" Peter hooted. "I've got the pictures to prove it."

Lucky looked at him with interest.

"Not here," Peter admitted. "They're at home. I've got at least a dozen."

"Send me one?" Lucky asked, and Sam looked at her askance.

"What could you possibly want that for?"

"Oh, I don't know," she said airily. "Blackmail?"

"You forget," said Sam. "I've seen your grade school yearbook."

Lucky swallowed a gulp of beer. "Oh, right." She smiled at Peter sweetly. "Cancel that order, would you?"

"Will do." Peter laughed, looking back and forth between them. "You know," he said finally, his gaze stopping on Sam. "She's good for you."

Lucky felt the beginnings of a blush and reached for a hasty sip of beer.

Without missing a beat, Peter turned laughing eyes her way. "You should have seen some of his other dates."

"Peter!" Sam intoned. They both decided to ignore him.

"Pretty?" asked Lucky.

"Hard to tell. Most of them were stiff as boards."

"I'll tell your sister you said so," Sam announced and Peter yelped in outrage.

"You never dated my sister!"

"Oh no?" Sam's voice was silky smooth. "What about that summer we spent working at that resort on Cape Cod?"

They were still arguing the point, the discussion punctuated by loud and frequent laughter, when the last of the pizza disappeared. "Now what?" Lucky asked, when they'd finished putting everything away.

"Ice cream!" cried Peter, snatching up Sam's car keys. "It's on me."

"After all that food?" Lucky groaned.

"Best thing for you," Peter announced. "Good for the digestion."

"Does he ever sit still for a moment?" she asked in a loud stage whisper.

"Not since I've known him," Sam replied. "It's probably best just to give in and go along gracefully."

"Look at that," Peter teased. "And here I thought you were too old to learn something new." He fielded Sam's mock punch and herded them toward the door.

By the time they reached the Häagen-Dazs store, Peter was singing nursery rhymes. On the way home, it was elephant jokes. Lucky laughed until her sides ached, and when Peter threatened to moon a passing police car, for a moment she almost thought he'd do it. At the last minute good sense prevailed, and they managed to get themselves home without incident.

Though it was after midnight before Lucky left, she was sorry the evening had to end. She felt heartened by what she had seen, and curiously reassured. On the surface, Peter and Sam had little in common, yet their friendship had spanned more than a dozen years. Was she dreaming, she wondered, to believe that she and Sam could have a future, too?

## 11

"THAT'S ONE." Lucky said with satisfaction. She and Sam were standing beside a twenty-year-old Mercedes Benz 280SL. Purchased several days earlier, it had just been delivered to her lot by a tow truck. "It'll make a perfect beginning."

"I'm glad you think so." Sam leaned down to look inside the sports car and immediately regretted the move. The dashboard was worn and pitted, and the bucket seats had been covered by a pair of ratty sheepskin rugs. "This car looks more like the end to me."

"I'll admit it does need a little work."

"A little?"

"Okay, maybe a lot." Lucky ran a hand lightly over the roof of the car, her fingers stroking the faded paint as though consoling the little sedan for its condition. "But that's what we're in business for."

"I know," said Sam. Her sales pitch was still fresh in his mind. "Restoring old cars to their former glory."

Lucky shot him a look. "If it was perfect already, there wouldn't be any profit in it for us, now would there?"

"Just how much profit do you expect to find in a two-thousand-dollar Mercedes Benz?"

"Trust me. By the time we're finished, this'll be a twenty thousand dollar car. Easy."

Sam smiled at the cockiness in Lucky's tone, enjoying her enthusiasm, her optimism and the sheer exhilaration that shone in her tawny brown eyes. It was a combination that never failed to give him pleasure.

Arranging their schedules to afford them more time together had proven more of a chore than either had anticipated. In the past ten days, however, they'd fallen into the routine of lunching together during the week—a routine that was working remarkably well.

Sam had learned from past experience that there was only so much time he could spend with one woman before growing either claustrophobic or bored. He had wondered at first whether so much togetherness would simply accelerate the pace of their relationship and drive it ever faster toward an inevitable ending. But if his time with Lucky had shown him anything, it was that nothing was inevitable.

Day by day she continued to surprise and delight him until he'd come to the conclusion that of all the possibilities open to them, boredom was not even on the list. Once, when Lucky was unavailable, he'd been jolted by the realization that he'd come to count on their routine, to think of their lunches as a welcome oasis in the middle of his often long days.

She was beginning to matter to him in ways he wouldn't have thought possible only a few short months ago. He'd never allowed himself to depend on anyone else before; he hadn't thought he'd allowed it now. But Lucky's presence had begun to permeate his life the same way her image haunted him when they were apart.

Slowly but surely, she was chipping away at his defenses. And for once Sam, who'd always thought of himself as a decisive man, had no idea how to respond. Half of him wanted to run like hell; the other half was more than a little tempted to pitch in and give her a hand.

Standing beside the car, Lucky shaded her face with her hand and gazed at Sam speculatively. She'd grown accus-

tomed to his occasional silences, respecting his preference
to think things through, rather than say whatever crossed
his mind as she was so often apt to do. Now, however, he
didn't look preoccupied so much as worried.

"Thinking about your investment?" she inquired softly.

"No, not at all." Sam shook his head, clearing his
thoughts. "I'm sure the car will do fine. Why don't you have
Clem get to work on the engine and I'll send over a couple
of my men in a day or two to look at the transmission."

"Sounds good." Lucky fingered a crick in the sports car's
antenna. "I won't be here, but I'll tell Clem to expect them."

Sam turned in surprise, then abruptly remembered. "Oh
yes, the wedding everyone was discussing at the barbecue.
How long will you be gone?"

Interesting, thought Lucky. She ought to be bridling at
his proprietary tone. Instead she found she was rather
pleased. "Through next Monday."

"That long?"

"Umm-hmm." Abruptly Lucky flinched as the brittle
metal she was straightening broke off in her hand. Then she
saw Sam's grimace and smiled. "Don't worry, I'll add it to
the list. As to the wedding, you know it's not too late to
change your mind and come with me."

Sam gave the idea a moment's thought, but finally shook
his head. "Somehow I think I'm better off learning to deal
with the Vanderholdens in slightly smaller doses than a
family wedding that size would entail. Besides, four days is
more than I can spare right now. How about you, you're not
closing down, are you?"

"Are you kidding?"

"That's what I thought." Sam was pleased he'd read her
so well. "If you like, I can send over one of my salesmen to
mind the store while you're gone."

"One of *your* salesmen working at Lucky's-Late Model Lovelies?" Lucky arched a brow. "Whoever he is, he'd be furious!"

"Not if he knew what was good for him."

A month ago Sam never would even have considered making such an offer, much less leaped to her lot's defense. With a small start of pleasure she realized that her business had finally acquired a legitimacy in his eyes that it hadn't possessed before. It only went to prove how far they'd come.

"Thanks for the offer, but really there's no need. There's a man—a moonlighting college professor actually—who provides backup for me whenever I'm away. He's gathering material for a book and claims to have found some of my customers absolutely fascinating. I'm sure he'd be crushed if I put him out of work."

"Fine, I'm glad you're all set." Sam listened to his own words and frowned. They didn't convey at all what he'd meant to say. "I hope you have a good time," he added, trying again. The meaning was closer, but still not quite right.

"Thanks, I'm sure I will."

"Give your family my best."

Lucky bit back a smile. She'd never watched Sam squirm before. It was, she found, an interesting experience. "I'll do that, too." She waited a beat, then asked, "Anything else?"

"Yes, there's something else!"

Eyes dancing, Lucky tilted her face to his. Sam reached up to cup it in his hands. "I'll miss you," he said softly.

Lucky lifted her hands and covered his. Even though his reasons were valid, Lucky still couldn't help regretting that Sam hadn't changed his mind and decided to accompany her. "I'll miss you, too."

"You'd better," Sam growled, surprised by his own ve-
hemence.

"Bet on it." The quiet words were followed by an even
softer sigh.

AS LUCKY HAD EXPECTED, her cousin's wedding was a riot-
ous affair. A rough count revealed that over half of the two
hundred guests were relatives of one connection or another. And if there was one thing the Vanderholden family
knew how to do, it was have a good time. As a member of
the wedding party, Lucky was put to work the moment she
arrived. Between fittings, rehearsals and a last minute
shower that turned into an all-night party, she scarcely had
a moment to herself. Not that Lucky was complaining.
Business had been so good lately she felt she'd neglected her
family shamelessly. Now she used the long weekend to
touch base with each of her relatives and catch up on the
latest gossip.

Still, it was with some relief that Lucky turned her car into
her own driveway late Monday evening. The wedding had
been a complete success, and from all indications, the marriage would be, as well. The newlyweds were on their way
to Bermuda, she'd just dropped Ken off at his dorm at Vil-
lanova, and she was eager to get back to her usual routine.

After a good night's sleep, Lucky arrived at her office the
next morning feeling refreshed and ready for anything.
She'd just sat down at her desk when she heard the sound
of a car pulling up outside. Tossing her purse into a bottom
drawer, she looked up expectantly.

A moment later the door swung open to admit a slender
young man with thick tortoiseshell glasses and an unruly
shock of sandy-colored hair. He stepped into the office, then
paused to look around.

Lucky had a knack for sizing people up quickly, a talent that had been honed by her years in sales. Now, unless her first impression was mistaken, this man—not much more than a teenager, really—would rather be just about anywhere else than where he was. Quickly she moved to put him at ease.

"I'm Lucky Vanderholden." Her smile was warm as she stood and extended her hand. "How can I help you?"

"Um, I read your ad." He stared at her hand blankly for a moment, then brushed his palm on the leg of his pants before grasping her fingers for a quick shake. "I'm Dewey Phillips."

"Nice to meet you, Dewey." Lucky gestured toward a chair. "Would you like to sit down?"

"Yes, I guess so." The chair scraped across the floor as he pulled it up in front of her desk.

"I have several ads running at the moment, which one did you read?"

Dewey nudged his glasses back up the bridge of his nose and squinted at her hopefully. "The one that said you're buying old cars. You know, top prices paid?"

Lucky leaned her elbows on either side of her blotter and braced her fingers in a steeple. "Yes," she said slowly, "I am interested in acquiring cars. However, I'm not looking for old cars, but rather for certain classic models."

"Oh, my car's a classic all right!" Abruptly Dewey's face lit with enthusiasm, and the transformation was nothing short of astonishing. "A 1956 Thunderbird. It's got a V8 engine, 202 horsepower, convertible and hardtop roofs—"

"Whoa!" Lucky held up a hand to stop the flow of words. "The car does sound wonderful, exactly like what I'm looking for. When can I see it?"

"Right now. I've got it outside."

"You mean it runs too?"

"Of course it runs," Dewey said with pride. "Wouldn't be much of a car if it didn't."

No sooner had Lucky stepped out onto the tarmac than she saw that Dewey's car was everything he had promised, and more. Low and sleek, with porthole windows and a spare tire mounted vertically above the rear bumper, the cream colored Thunderbird was a classic-car buff's dream.

She let out a long sigh, then turned in wonder. "You really want to sell *that*?"

"Sure," Dewey said defensively. "I wouldn't be here otherwise, would I?"

Something wasn't quite right, Lucky realized, watching the conflicting emotions that crossed Dewey's expressive face. When he talked about the car, his features came alive, but whenever he mentioned selling it, all signs of animation vanished. There was more to the story than she'd learned so far, and Lucky was determined to find out what it was.

"If you don't mind," she said, "I'll have my mechanic take a look while we step into my office and talk."

"Sure," Dewey agreed. Clem was called from the garage, and Dewey handed over the keys before taking a last, lingering look at the Thunderbird and following Lucky inside.

"Now then," she said, pulling out a piece of paper on which to make notes. "Where did you get the car?"

"From my father." Dewey fingered the seam in his pants absently.

"Then it was a gift?"

"A bequest actually, my father's dead." Dewey glanced up as a thought struck him. "You don't have to worry, the title's clear."

Lucky nodded and made a note in the margin. "When did your father purchase the car?"

"In 1956, straight from a dealer. He had to save for three years before he got enough money together, but he always said it was worth it."

Lucky's brows drew together in a frown. "The car's been in your family for over thirty years."

"Yeah." Dewey ducked his head. "Longer than me."

"But you still want to sell it?"

"Yeah, sure. That's why I'm here."

"You don't look very happy about the situation."

His shoulders rose and fell in a helpless shrug. "I don't have much choice. My mom's sick. I need the money."

Lucky made another note on the paper before her as Clem stuck his head in the open door and gave her a silent "thumbs up." She nodded her thanks, then turned back to Dewey. All at once he looked a great deal younger than his years. Much as she wanted to have the Thunderbird, she realized that she wanted him to keep it more.

"Is this the only way you can think of to raise money?" she asked quietly. "What about your job, is there a credit union where you work?"

Dewey looked up, surprised by the question. "Believe me, if there was any other way. . ." He shook his head in resignation. "The problem is I work freelance—you know, designing computer software? I'm doing okay, actually pretty well. And I've just developed this new package—" once again, Dewey was fired with enthusiasm "—when it sells, it's going to go through the roof. We're negotiating the rights now."

"Maybe the people you're dealing with would be willing to give you an advance?" Lucky suggested kindly. She saw elements of Ken in the earnest young man sitting before her, and of Hal, too. Suddenly it seemed far more important to help him out than to strike a deal.

"Not until we sign the contracts, and that might not be for weeks. My mom can't wait that long."

"I see."

"I was thinking, though—" Dewey looked at her hopefully "—maybe once the software sales goes through, I could come back. I mean, there's no reason I couldn't buy the car back myself, is there?"

"No," Lucky said slowly, "provided it's still here." She didn't feel the need to mention that a car as beautiful as Dewey's Thunderbird was not likely to last long on the open market.

"Well, then, you see? Maybe everything will work out after all."

For Dewey's sake, Lucky summoned a smile. "Maybe it will. Now, let's get down to business."

Sensing Dewey was a novice when it came to negotiating, she named what she felt was a fair price for the car and within minutes, the deal had been struck. Lucky wrote out a check, then watched as Dewey said goodbye to the Thunderbird before walking to the corner to catch a bus. When she turned back to her office, Clem was standing behind her.

"Car needs some work," he said. "Not much. You want to put a rush on it, I can—"

"No, don't bother." Lucky shook her head decisively. "I have a feeling that one's going to be on the lot for a while."

"Not that little beauty. She'll be out of here in no time flat."

"Maybe," Lucky said thoughtfully. "Maybe not."

Late in the morning she put in a call to Donahue Motors to see if Sam was free for lunch. After four days away, she couldn't wait to see him again. To her surprise, however, when the switchboard put through the connection, she found herself talking not to Sam but to Joe Saks.

"Sam asked me to fill you in if you called," he said.

"Is something wrong?"

"Sam's sick with some sort of bug. He called in yesterday and said he'd be out for a couple days."

Lucky frowned, immediately concerned. "It's nothing serious, is it?"

"No, probably just the flu. He asked me to tell you that he'd give you a call when he was up and around again."

"When he's up and around again? Who's taking care of him in the meantime?"

"Take it from somebody who knows, Sam's a real bear when he's sick. He doesn't *want* anyone taking care of him."

"Well, we'll just see about that," Lucky muttered. No sooner had the dial tone begun to buzz in her ear than she was making plans.

After work she shopped, cooked and packed a basket of supplies. By seven o'clock she was ready to make a condolence call. At Sam's condo she rang the doorbell, then, when there was no answer, she knocked loudly and called out, "Sam? It's me, Lucky."

Several minutes passed before Lucky heard the sound of locks being released. The door opened a crack and Sam's face appeared. He looked pale, bleary-eyed, and not particularly pleased to see her. "I'm sick," he announced. "Didn't you talk to Joe?"

"Of course, that's why I'm here." Lucky braced a palm against the door and pushed. It didn't budge. "Aren't you going to let me in?"

"No." Another time, his voice might have been adamant. Now he merely sounded disgruntled.

"How do you expect to get better if there's nobody taking care of you?"

"The same way I always do," Sam said slowly as if the mere act of speaking at all was an effort. "I'll stay in bed and sweat it out."

"Nonsense. I've brought you some juice and my special homemade soup. At least let me deliver the food to your kitchen."

He shook his head. "I don't feel well enough to eat."

"Then I'll just—"

"Lucky!" Sam cast her a baleful look. "I hate having company when I'm sick."

"Perfect, so do I. Don't think of me as company. Think of me as a nurse."

"I don't need a nurse—"

This time the shove she gave the door caught him by surprise. It gave another six inches, just enough for her to slip inside.

"Has anybody ever told you you're a very pushy woman?" Sam demanded.

"Several people. I try not to let it go to my head."

Now that she was finally able to see all of him, Lucky realized with a start that the extent of Sam's attire was a pair of pajama bottoms that had slipped below his waist to cling precariously to his lean hips. As he turned and headed back down the hall, she stared openly, giving his body the full measure of appreciation it deserved.

Sam sneezed heartily, jolting Lucky back to the matter at hand. "You realize I'm probably contagious," he grumbled.

"I'll take my chances."

"You'll have to." Sam paused in the doorway to his bedroom. "As far as I'm concerned, you're on your own. I'm in no shape to do any entertaining."

"So who asked you to?" Lucky muttered. As she strode down the hall toward the kitchen a glance in the open door to Sam's bedroom revealed that he was climbing back into bed.

No wonder Joe'd called him a bear, she thought, unloading her supplies on the counter. Grizzly was more like it. Lucky poured some soup into a bowl and set it in the microwave to heat. Then she pulled out a glass and filled it to the brim with juice.

Despite Sam's protests, she refused to believe that a bit of loving care wouldn't make him feel a good deal more comfortable. It had always worked for her. Indeed she had rather fond memories of being sick when she was little, the whole family rallying around to try and make her feel better. And if loving care didn't work, Lucky mused, well there was always the curative value of her mother's miracle chicken soup.

She found a tray beneath the counter and set a meal consisting of warm soup, cool juice and a plateful of crackers. She'd taken no more than two steps inside Sam's room, however, when he opened one eye and stated firmly, "I'm not hungry."

"That's what you think." Lucky set the tray on a side table and picked up several pillows to brace behind his back. "Sit up."

"Do I have to?"

"Yes."

"Nobody asked you to play Florence Nightingale," Sam grumbled as he raised himself to a sitting position.

"Nobody asked you to act like you were five years old, either, but that doesn't seem to be stopping you." Lucky plopped the tray down in his lap. "Now eat!"

"Your bedside manner could use some work."

"So could yours," Lucky returned sweetly. "Try the soup."

Sam gazed down at the bowl dubiously. "I don't like soup."

"Fine." She thrust a spoon into his hands. "Fake it."

"You don't really believe that old saw about chicken soup curing all your ills, do you?"

She did, but that was beside the point. "I haven't lost a patient yet."

"I can see why. You make being sick so unpalatable, people would probably do anything to get well."

Lucky bit back a sharp retort as Sam dipped the spoon into the soup and began to eat. He could be as insulting as he wanted as long as she got some nourishment into him.

It was a measure of how truly weak Sam was that it took him almost fifteen minutes to consume the bowl of soup and half a glass of juice. As Lucky lifted the tray away and readjusted the pillows, he collapsed down onto them wearily. "Get some rest," she said. "I'll check in on you in a little while."

"Mmm." Sam agreed, his eyes already shut. "Lucky?"

She paused on her way to the door.

"Thanks."

The single word made it all worthwhile, Lucky realized as she cleaned up the dinner dishes, then sat down in the living room to thumb through a magazine. It wasn't Sam's fault he wasn't used to being cared for, any more than it was hers that she couldn't help caring.

An hour later when she peeked in, he was sleeping quietly. An hour after that, however, he had thrown off the covers, discarded the pillow, and was tossing fitfully. She entered the room and laid a hand on his brow. He was burning up with fever.

Lucky hurried into the bathroom and slid open the medicine cabinet. There was a bottle of aspirin on the lower shelf. She shook out two pills, then poured a glass of cold water to go with them. When she returned to the bedroom, Sam was half awake and groaning softly.

"I've got some pills for you to take," Lucky slipped an arm around his shoulders and helped him into an upright position.

"What are they?"

"Aspirin, straight from your own medicine cabinet." She supported his back while Sam tossed the pills into his mouth and swallowed them with a quick gulp of water. Then she eased him back down onto the bed.

"Sorry I'm not a better host," Sam muttered vaguely.

If he hadn't looked so out of sorts, Lucky would have smiled. "Don't worry. You're doing fine."

"I feel rotten."

"I know." Lucky's voice was soft, soothing. "You just lie there and wait for the aspirin to take affect. In the meantime I'm going to get a cold compress for your forehead."

There were linens in a cupboard beside the sink and Lucky pulled out a washcloth and saturated it with cold water. As she stepped from the lighted bathroom into the darkness of the bedroom, Sam was no more than a shadowy figure in the middle of the bed. Then her eyes adjusted and he slowly swam into focus.

He lay back upon the pillows, his eyes closed, his hair a dark contrast to the pale blue linens. One arm had been flung up over his head, the other rested across his chest, fingers curled around the edge of the sheet. Lucky smiled softly as a wave of tenderness washed through her. In repose, Sam lost the hard edges he sometimes turned toward the world. Half awake, half asleep, he looked both vulnerable and unutterably weary.

He needed her whether he knew it or not. This big, strong, independent man actually needed her help. The thought was both gratifying and more than a little humbling.

With gentle fingers, she laid the cold towel across his forehead. Sam sighed softly, but didn't open his eyes. Sitting on the edge of his bed, Lucky watched as, gradually, the hot color in his cheeks began to fade and his ragged breathing became more regular. His hair was damp, and Lucky smoothed the strands up off his forehead, her fingers tangling in the shiny silk.

"Talk to me," Sam murmured.

Lucky bit back a smile. "You want to hear a bedtime story?"

"Hardly." One eye slipped open. "Tell me about your day."

Though he didn't seem in much shape to care, Lucky was happy to oblige him. Perched on the edge of the mattress, she recounted the story of Dewey Phillips and the beautiful Thunderbird that was now sitting out in the back of her lot. "The only thing is," she said at the end, "we can't sell the car. I mean, we can, but not yet. If you'd seen the way Dewey felt about that car . . . We just have to give him enough time to get back on his feet."

"Sounds like a good idea," Sam muttered sleepily.

"I'm glad you agree."

It took only a few more minutes before Sam had drifted off. When at last he was sleeping soundly, Lucky leaned down and brushed a light kiss across the side of his cheek. The day's stubble tickled her lips and she laughed softly as she gazed down upon him. *So this is what it feels like to be consumed by love,* she thought. *To look at a man and know that you want to spend the rest of your life with him.*

Sam stirred, turning on his side to face the other way.

"Ingrate," Lucky whispered good-naturedly. She rose from the bed and tiptoed from the room, shutting the door behind her.

THE NEXT MORNING, Lucky stopped by to check on Sam on her way to work. This time when he met her at the door, he was much steadier on his feet. Though he still went back to bed after letting her in, it was clear he was feeling much better.

"I see you didn't bring any more soup," he said with satisfaction as Lucky followed him into the bedroom.

"There's still plenty left from last night," she informed him, opening the shades to let in some light.

"I'll bet."

Lucky's brow rose. "Are you disputing the efficiency of my miracle cure?"

"Flus run a course. This one almost has."

"I see." Lucky reached around behind him, plumping up the pillows to arrange them more comfortably.

"Cut it out, would you?" Sam's hand reached out to capture hers.

Lucky looked down at him in surprise. "Cut what out?"

"This, all of it. The fussing, the cooking. Can't you just let me be sick in peace?"

Lucky thought about that for a long moment. She thought about her love for Sam, which had shimmered so brightly the night before. Then she tucked it away, deep down inside where he would never guess at its existence.

"No," she said finally. "I can't."

Sam glared up at her from his semi-prone position. "I can take care of myself."

"Of course you can. That's why you were looking so chipper when I arrived last evening."

"Stop sounding like little Mary Sunshine. Don't you have to go to work or something?"

"I'm on my way there now."

Sam stared at the door pointedly. "I wouldn't want to make you late."

"All right, all right." Lucky tossed up her hands in defeat. "I'm going."

He'd gotten what he wanted, so why did he suddenly feel like such a heel? Granted, his efforts at rejection had been somewhat less than subtle, but with Lucky in this nurturing mode of hers, nothing short of outright rudeness seemed to make a dent in her determination.

"It just kills you, doesn't it?"

Sam looked up, surprised. Lucky was standing outside the door to his bedroom. "What?"

"Having to depend on someone else, even just a little."

If all his faculties had been humming along at full power, he'd have been able to deliver a decent comeback. As it was, he was still trying to think of a clever retort when he heard the outer door to his apartment close. Could he help it if he was used to being in charge of his own life?

Ever since Lucky had run those ridiculous commercials of hers, she'd been caroming through his affairs with all the energy of a high-power rocket gone amok. She'd teased him with cake, tempted him with classic cars, and tantalized him with that lithe body of hers until there were times when he didn't know if he was coming or going. Could he be blamed for wanting to step in and reassert some measure of control?

Perhaps not. But he could be blamed for snapping and snarling unnecessarily when, even to him, it was clear that Lucky was only trying to help. That was the difference between them. When he saw a problem, he stepped back, considered the situation, then tried to work things through logically. Lucky, on the other hand, simply dove in head first.

The last time she'd tried to lend him a hand, he'd let his car come between them, Sam mused. This time he had no intention of making a similar mistake. Tonight he'd apologize and set things right. He had the rest of the day to figure out how.

# 12

LUCKY SPENT the whole morning congratulating herself on her decision not to return to Sam's apartment after work—and the whole afternoon calling herself a fool because she knew she was going back anyway.

A truly liberated woman would have told Sam Donahue to go jump in a lake, Lucky told herself firmly as she closed up her office and headed out. Then again, a little voice asked, what truly liberated woman would know by heart the recipe for Mom's miracle chicken soup? The problem was that she'd been born to get involved. And right now, she was going to make sure Sam got well if it killed him!

This time Lucky didn't have to ring the bell. The door to Sam's apartment was standing slightly ajar. Calling out his name, she let herself in.

"Be right there." He emerged from the kitchen at the end of the hall, dressed in a faded polo shirt and a pair of snug-fitting jeans. His hair was damp, his jaw freshly shaven. There was spring in his step and, if Lucky wasn't mistaken, a rakishly seductive gleam in his eye.

The transformation seemed to call for some sort of comment, but for a brief, startled moment Lucky could only stand and stare. Then Sam was upon her, taking her purse from her hand and laying it on the table before gathering her in his arms for a welcoming kiss.

When he finally released her, she was breathless as well as speechless. "You're up," she managed finally.

"That's what I like about you, Lucky." Sam grinned, taking her hand and leading her toward the kitchen. "You're quick."

"But last night," Lucky found herself sputtering, and realized she had no idea whether her confusion was due to surprise at his remarkable recovery or the sudden shaft of desire produced by his tousled, and undeniably sexy, appearance. "Last night, you looked like you were on death's doorstep."

Sam's large hands clasped either side of her waist, lifting her up and depositing her atop one of the stools beside the counter. "It was a forty-eight-hour bug. My time was up."

Still bemused, Lucky watched as Sam opened the refrigerator and leaned down to pull out a large bowl filled with crisp salad. The movement molded the soft denim of his jeans tightly over his firm buttocks. Unexpectedly, her stomach muscles clenched.

"Then if you're all better..." Lucky pushed the words out. "I guess you really don't need me here."

Sam straightened and slowly turned to face her. His eyes, dark and smoldering, found hers. "I wouldn't say that."

"This morning—"

Sam's frown was quick and self-deprecating. "This morning I acted like an ass."

"Yes." Lucky watched as his foot hooked the refrigerator door behind him and nudged it shut. "You did."

"Tonight, I'm hoping you'll forgive me."

Lucky took her time about answering. Clearly Sam wanted her to stay. With a shaft of pure pleasure, Lucky realized that there was nothing that she wanted more. "Consider it done," she said, then peered over the counter top toward the stove and deliberately changed the subject. "Did you cook?"

Sam dipped a wooden spoon into a large pot on the back burner, then held it to Lucky's lips so she could sample the sauce. "I hope you don't mind pasta again. It's all I had in the freezer."

"I never mind pasta." Lucky sniffed the air. "Garlic bread?"

"Only if you'll agree to join me."

"I'll be happy to. Does it matter?"

"Definitely." Sam's hand reached out across the counter, his fingers trailing softly up and down the length of her bare arm. Goose bumps rose, then merged until her entire body was tingling with his touch. "I wouldn't dream of kissing you otherwise."

"Are you planning . . ." Lucky's voice was breathy, tremulous. She cleared her throat and tried again. "Are you planning on kissing me?"

"Lucky," Sam growled softly. "I'm counting on it."

Somehow they managed to get the food onto the plates and the plates onto the table. Salad was served, then remained untouched in their bowls. The garlic bread lay forgotten in the oven until it had burned to a crisp. Sam and Lucky couldn't have cared less. They only had eyes for each other.

With infinite care, Sam twirled a forkful of spaghetti and held it up to Lucky's lips. The tip of her tongue guided the morsel inside, and she smiled as she began to chew. "Wonderful," she said blissfully.

"Yes," Sam agreed. His eyes roved lazily over Lucky's creamy throat and the smooth skin exposed by her V-neck top, leaving little doubt as to what he was referring to.

She sighed softly, delighting in the intensity with which Sam focused his attention upon her. She had never felt so catered to before, nor so desired. It was a heady combination, lighting fires deep within her that rose and swirled until her head was awhirl with anticipation.

Lucky took another bite and chewed slowly. "Delicious."

"Mmm." Sam lifted her hand and kissed each of her fingers in turn. "That, too."

With deliberate care, Lucky laid her fork on the side of her plate and reached for a sip of wine. The Pinot Noir was deep and rich, and its fruity flavor lingered on her lips. Her tongue flicked out and grazed their soft outline, savoring the last drops. When she looked up, she saw that Sam had missed nothing. His own lips were slightly parted, his breathing deep and uneven.

"You're not eating," Lucky pointed out.

"Suddenly I'm not hungry."

Neither was she, thought Lucky. Not when she had the sexiest man in the world sitting two feet away looking at her as though she was the most desirable woman he'd ever seen. She inhaled deeply, and the breath seemed to catch in her throat. Her breasts swelled, nipples jutting against the lacy fabric that restrained them.

She turned her hand in his, her fingertips dancing lightly over the sensitive skin of his inner wrist. "Are you sure you've got your strength back?"

His answer was a low, husky, supremely confident laugh. "Try me."

His words, his laugh and the mesmerizing look in Sam's eyes all combined to set Lucky's senses afire. She felt surrounded by Sam's presence, enmeshed in the evocative spell he had woven around them. Heat gathered, low and heavy, in her loins. Her limbs felt weak, languorous; yet at the same time, the sound of her own heartbeat pounded in her ears. And still they were barely touching.

"Sam . . . ?" Lucky murmured wonderingly.

He rose to his feet. The hand that clasped hers drew her up beside him and into his arms. Lucky's hands ran up the sides of his chest and around the back of his neck as Sam's lips came down to hers. Her mouth was open and eager, her body throbbing with need.

Sam's fingers tangled in her hair, holding her to him as he plundered her mouth with his tongue. She tasted of wine, her soft mouth yielding, taking, absorbing his thrusts then meeting them with her own. Pleasure rose like a golden mist, and the world around them seemed to dissolve, reduced to nothing save their two bodies and the friction that sparked between them.

Sam had never felt the way he did when he was with Lucky, never needed with an urgency that overwhelmed everything save its own desire for release.

His hand spanned the back of Lucky's waist, drawing her closer. His thigh slipped between hers and she rubbed against him sinuously, moaning softly. Her breasts flattened against his chest, and Sam felt the heavy weight of their fullness, felt the stiff points of her nipples inviting his sweet caress.

Lucky had known there'd be an explosion when they touched, but nothing could have prepared her for this. The yearning that had filled her earlier was nothing compared to the reckless, fiery passion that consumed her now. She wanted Sam, all of him, on top of her, inside of her. She'd never be satisfied until he'd filled her with his heat as surely as he'd filled her with this exquisite need.

"This way," Sam murmured, his lips so close that Lucky felt the warmth of his breath upon her neck. Her eyes slipped open questioningly, and he smiled. "Otherwise we're going to find ourselves on the kitchen floor in a minute or two."

It only took them a moment to reach the bedroom where Sam had changed the sheets and half drawn the shades. Light and dark played across the room, the shadows punctuated by the last glow of the setting sun. Lucky followed several steps into the room, then paused.

Waiting by the bed, Sam held out a hand. "Come to me, Lucky."

It was all the invitation she needed. Lucky flowed into Sam's arms, her face tilting up to his like a flower reaching toward the sun. Her fingers hastened down the front of his shirt, unfastening each button in turn, then easing the soft cotton from his shoulders and letting it fall to the floor at their feet.

"You have the most beautiful body," she murmured, her teeth nipping playfully at the angled curve of his shoulder. "Last night, when you answered the door..." Lucky moaned softly. "If you hadn't been so sick, I'd have been all over you."

Sam chuckled huskily. "If I hadn't felt so awful, I'd have beaten you to it. Do you know how many times I looked at my watch while you were away last weekend? How many times I reached for the phone? How tempted I was to get in my car, drive to Scarsdale and bring you home?"

Lucky grinned wickedly. Her fingers skimmed across his stomach and felt his muscles tighten. "You'd have scandalized all the wedding guests."

"Maybe." Sam's hands slipped beneath the lower edge of Lucky's top, lifting it up and over her head. His gaze roved downward greedily, taking in the sight of her firm breasts, swollen with desire and spilling out over the cups of her filmy bra. "But would I have scandalized you?"

"Never." Lucky tossed her head, golden curls swirling around her face seductively. "I'd have loved it."

And she would have, Lucky realized suddenly. As important as her family was to her, Sam was more so. And strong as her feelings for her relatives were, they couldn't approach the depth of emotion she felt for Sam.

Her fingers slid downward. The waistband of his jeans was tight, the fabric below it tighter still. Her hand lingered, then began to rub. Groaning, Sam thrust forward until she cupped his rigid strength.

"Lucky!" Sam gasped. "Do you have any idea what you're doing to me?"

"Mmm," Lucky murmured. It was part answer, part sigh of appreciation.

There was a soft whir as Sam slid down the zipper to her skirt. He hooked his thumbs in the waistband, and skirt and slip slid down together to land in a pool on the floor. Lucky stepped out of her shoes and stood before him, naked save for two lacy wisps of underwear.

"You take my breath away." Sam's hands lifted to the front of her bra, unfastening the clasp and smoothing the cups aside.

Her breasts were firm and creamy smooth, tipped by aureoles the color of dusky rose. He cradled them in his hands as his head lowered. Lucky felt the soft brush of his hair against her throat, saw the eagerness with which his tongue flicked out to touch one swollen tip, then threw her head back with a sudden, rapturous gasp as Sam drew the straining nipple into his mouth and sucked deeply.

A burst of sensation arrowed through her body like a jagged streak of lightning. Lucky's arms circled Sam's head, her hands stroking, tangling in his hair, urging him closer, and then closer still. Desire, strong and hot, spiraled within her, building until the tension was almost more than she could bear.

Her fingers flew to the snap of his jeans, clumsy in their haste as they unfastened the pants, then worked them down over Sam's hips. "Easy," he murmured, his breath warm on her skin. "We have all the time in the world."

But Lucky couldn't go slowly; all at once she hadn't the slightest idea how. She'd never felt like this before, incomplete, as though something vital was missing that could only be provided by the joining of Sam's body to her own. "I need you now," she whispered fiercely, and Sam groaned at the naked desire he read in her eyes.

The last of their underwear was pushed down and away, then Sam gathered Lucky in his arms and lowered her gently to the bed. He'd meant to take his time, to give them both a chance to adjust and find a rhythm all their own. But now he found his own pulse raging, yearning rocketing through him with a demanding greed that matched Lucky's own.

He settled his body above hers, eyes centered on her face as he thrust himself into her. She moaned, a primal sound that came from deep in her throat. Then her hands were sliding down the length of his back, her fingers grasping the firm muscles of his buttocks as she began to move beneath him.

Pleasure shuddered through him, the feeling so intense that his breath caught in his throat. He'd known passion before, but he'd never known that it was possible for his whole body to burn with such exquisite bliss. He'd known satisfaction, but never this joyous, overwhelming sense of completion. A tempest built and swirled within him, sensation eddying higher and higher.

The thunderous pounding of his heart was like a primitive, ritual beat, urging Lucky on. Their bodies moved in rhythm, hard and fast. She closed her eyes, held Sam close and went where he would take her.

She'd been waiting all her life for this moment, this man. Love shimmered at the edge of her consciousness as she felt her body begin to contract around him and spasms of ecstasy shot through her. Then Sam was there with her, driving furiously with a series of final pulsing thrusts. Lucky wrapped her arms around him and held on tight. Her embrace encompassed everything she'd ever wanted.

The moments passed slowly as they both floated back to earth. Gently Lucky's hands skimmed over Sam's sweat-soaked back. With equal tenderness his fingers tangled in her hair. When he shifted his weight to lie beside her, Lucky nestled in the crook of his arm. She lifted her eyes and their gazes met. As one, they both smiled.

"I love you, Sam," Lucky whispered dreamily. Then as the effect of the hectic weekend and the busy days that had followed since finally took its toll, she turned her face into his shoulder, closed her eyes and slept.

WHEN LUCKY AWOKE, the room was fully dark. She felt Sam's presence beside her, and when she turned, saw him lying propped up on one elbow, gazing down at her with a thoroughly bemused expression on his face.

"Have I been asleep long?" Lucky asked.

"Half an hour." Sam's fingers traced the line of her breastbone from shoulder to throat. "I enjoyed watching you."

Lucky grinned wickedly. "You enjoyed wearing me out."

"That, too."

He should have been smiling. Should have been basking complicitously in the delicious aftermath of what they had shared. But instead, his expression was intent, almost somber, as though there was something very serious on his mind. Slowly her grin faded.

Sam saw the change and reached up with his hand to stroke her shoulder reassuringly. Without thinking, Lucky drew back. She didn't want his reassurance, not now, not until she knew what was the matter.

"Did you mean what you said?" Sam asked quietly.

Lucky stared at him blankly. "When?"

"Earlier." This time Sam's hand, pulling her close, brooked no argument. "You told me you loved me."

"I do."

The bemused expression was back. And something else, Lucky realized, a flicker of emotion so real, so strong, that for a moment, a lump gathered in her throat.

"You make it sound so easy," said Sam.

"Isn't it?"

His first answer was a shrug. His second, as Lucky reached up to flick her tongue over the lobe of his ear, an indulgent chuckle. "You also make it very hard to think straight."

"Good." She nuzzled his lobe with her lips, then drew it into her mouth. "I've always thought that thinking straight was an overrated virtue."

Sam grasped her shoulders and set her gently away. "How about talking?"

"At the moment, I can think of better things to do."

"In a minute."

"You're very bossy all of a sudden."

"Call it a male prerogative."

"I didn't know males had any prerogatives."

"Lucky..." Sam drew her name out warningly. "I'm trying to be serious."

"Okay." Lucky plumped up her pillow and set it against the wall. As she sat up, the sheet dipped to her waist. She cast a complacent glance downward and let things fall where they may. "Go for it."

She'd done it on purpose, thought Sam, watching as her breasts, firm and round and incredibly enticing, bobbed sweetly at eye level. Involuntarily, his tongue reached out to moisten his dry lips. Go for it, indeed.

"You're a tease," he muttered as he drew himself up beside her.

"No I'm not," she informed him blithely. "A tease offers without any intention of following through, whereas I—"

"I know," Sam cut her off with a muttered oath. "Believe me, I know." He cast his eyes heavenward as though looking for divine intervention. "Lucky, we have to talk."

"I'm all ears."

What Groucho Marx could have done with an opening like that. With effort, Sam held to the topic at hand. "You and I are very different," he began.

"Thank goodness for small favors."

Sam quelled her with a glare. "You come from a large family. You're used to having other people around all the time. I'm not like that. All my life, I've been a bit of a loner. When people come too close..."

"Yes?"

Sam cleared his throat harshly. "In the past, I haven't had the time, and maybe not the inclination, to form many close relationships. I've always thought of them as a luxury, not a necessity."

Lucky tilted her face to his. "And now?"

"And now," Sam said softly, "I think I'm falling in love with you."

Lucky's heart swelled with emotion, the pleasure sharp and unbearably sweet. Still, there was something that wasn't quite right. "You don't look too happy about it."

"To tell you the truth, I'm not sure how I feel." The flat statement was honest, and disarmingly direct. "I guess it depends on where we go from here."

Lucky smiled. "Do we have to decide tonight?"

"Maybe not," Sam replied. "But like I said before, you and I are very different people, perhaps with two very different sets of expectations."

"I don't expect anything from you, Sam."

"No?"

"All I want," said Lucky, "is for us to be together."

"When, every day?"

"No—"

"Every other day?"

"Sam!" His name was a cry of desperation. "What's the matter with you?"

"Don't you see?" asked Sam. "To you, love means commitment."

"What's the matter with that?"

"Nothing, exactly."

Lucky leaned her head on Sam's shoulder. Her fingers slipped down to tangle in the soft sprinkling of hairs on his chest. "What does love mean to you?"

"That's precisely the problem. I've never been in love before, and I don't know. All I do know is that suddenly I feel cornered."

Lucky's hand stilled. "In other words, you want me and your independence, both."

"I don't know that I'd have put it in quite those terms."

"Then choose your own," Lucky invited. "I'm listening."

Sam's hand reached up to cover hers, his fingers warm and strong. "What I want is for us to slow down, to take things step by step, rather than rushing headlong into something we may both regret."

Whatever might happen between Sam and her, she'd never regret a minute of it, Lucky vowed. No matter how things turned out, she'd always cherish whatever time they had together. But that wasn't what Sam wanted to hear, and she knew it. No, he wanted reassurance that she wasn't about to start making guest lists and ordering flowers for the church. Deliberately she let her hand drift lower, her fingers spanning the flat of his stomach below his navel where the twisting curls of hair grew dark and dense.

She gave a husky purr, deep in her throat. "I'm willing to take it slowly if you are."

Sam's breath caught on a sudden gulp as her fingers curled around him. Abruptly his introspective mood vanished, replaced by far more elemental needs. "I'm willing," he growled, "to take it any way you like."

Sam's arms tightened around Lucky, crushing her to him. As his mouth captured hers, claiming it with a thrust of his tongue, she let go of thought and abandoned herself to sensation. For the time being, it was all she needed.

It wasn't until much later as Sam slept beside her in the dark and quiet room, that the questions they hadn't been able to answer returned. She'd always thought that love was everything. Now, Lucky realized, it just might not be enough.

# 13

LUCKY HAD ALWAYS THOUGHT of Cloverdale summers as long and hot, but now the time seemed to fly by. July came and went. Business, though seasonably slow, still moved in fits and starts.

By the end of the month, she and Sam had jointly purchased three more cars, and also sold their first—a Stutz Bearcat that went to a delighted collector—for a tidy profit. Deciding a celebration was in order, they drove to Philadelphia for a night on the town, enjoying the theater and then a midnight supper at a midtown café before winding up the evening at Lucky's. Inside the front door, Sam headed straight for the kitchen.

At a slower pace, Lucky followed along behind. She liked the way he looked in her house. She liked the ease with which he prowled through the small Victorian, as comfortable there now as if it was his own. There was a feeling of rightness, of belonging, as though his presence had become an indelible part of what went into making her house a home.

Not that she ever would have admitted as much to Sam. Without a doubt, that was the last thing he'd want to hear. Still, for all his protests and reservations, he'd managed to surprise her more than once. Well aware of her propensity to try too hard, Lucky had made a concerted effort to keep things low-key. Rather, it had been Sam who had ensured that they'd seen each other often, Sam who always seem to be calling, coming up with one reason or another for them to get together. Instead of reveling in the freedom she'd so conscientiously provided, he'd all but ignored it. And Lucky, for her part, couldn't have been happier.

And if she still felt doubts about their future, Lucky was much too practical to let them encroach on her enjoyment of what she and Sam were sharing now. Either Sam would come to feel as she did—that their relationship was as vital to his existence as the air he breathed—or he wouldn't. Either way, there was little she could do but give him the time and space he needed to decide for himself.

Entering the kitchen behind Sam, Lucky watched curiously as he opened the refrigerator and slid something out of the bottom shelf. "Correct me if I'm wrong," she said. "But aren't you the same man who, not very long ago, was too full to finish his own piece of cheesecake?"

Sam turned, his gray eyes twinkling. "I didn't say I was too full exactly, just that I wanted to share. Have I ever mentioned how much I enjoy watching you eat?"

"Mmm." Lucky smiled. "But you can tell me again."

"Better yet, you can show me again." Sam held up a chilled bottle of Perrier Jouet.

"Champagne?"

"One of the best."

Lucky cast a glance at her refrigerator. As far as she knew, it had never harbored a hidden stash of high-priced champagne. "Where did it come from?"

"I slipped it in there earlier while you were upstairs getting ready." He grasped the wire covering and twisted until it lifted off.

"What a perfectly wonderful idea." As Lucky pulled two flutes out of the cupboard and rinsed them off, Sam hooked his thumbs under the lip of the cork and expelled it gently. Leaving him to pour, she ducked into the den and emerged moments later with a gaily wrapped box.

"I have something for you, too."

Sam looked at the gift in surprise. "You shouldn't have."

"What's a celebration without presents?"

"I don't know," Sam teased. "What *is* a celebration without presents?"

"Dull." Lucky accepted the glass he held out to her and raised it to her lips. Bubbles rose to tickle her nose and lips. She sipped, then swallowed slowly. The champagne was dry and smooth as silk, and she expressed her appreciation with a sigh.

Sam felt himself grow warm with pleasure. "I'm glad you like it."

Lucky slid her arm through his and led him into the den, where they sat, side by side, on the couch. "I think you're spoiling me," she admitted, then held up a hand when he started to protest. "But don't stop, I love it."

"I'm not about to stop." Sam ran a hand along the back of the cushion. His fingers brushed lightly over her nape. "I was only going to point out that you're spoiling me, too."

"Me?" Lucky looked at him in surprise. "How?"

"In every way that matters," Sam said quietly.

To his consternation, he saw that she still looked unconvinced. Was it possible she didn't realize how much of a difference she'd made in his life? Could she really be unaware of the extent to which her blithe, light-hearted attitude had brightened his own outlook? She made him think, she made him laugh, and she made him feel—and he treasured all three equally. Indeed, Sam reflected, spoiling seemed entirely too tame a word for the gifts she'd given him. . . .

"Aren't you going to open your present?"

Sam lifted the beribboned box that sat on the table in front of them and grinned with childlike relish. He slid off the bow and set it carefully aside. Then, as Lucky watched in amusement, he untaped the paper with equal deliberation.

"Nothing like diving right in," she said.

"Hasn't anyone ever told you that the suspense is half the fun?"

"No," Lucky said firmly. "Tearing into it is half the fun."

Ignoring her prodding, Sam unfolded the wrapping paper and pulled it free. Underneath he found a small rectangular box bearing a picture of a camera on the front. He gazed at it for a moment, then slowly opened the lid.

"I told you you didn't have enough pictures. Now you can take your own. I even put in a roll of film to get you started."

"Thank you," Sam said softly, staring at the box in his lap. He hadn't even known that he wanted a camera, but now that it was there, he found that nothing could have pleased him more. With a pang, he realized that in some ways Lucky seemed almost to know him better than he knew himself. Then he pushed the thought aside and leaned back, looking through the viewfinder and aiming the lens. "Smile."

Lucky did, and the flashbulb popped, half blinding them both.

"I can see I'm going to need some practice," Sam said ruefully.

"Lots of practice," Lucky teased. "Maybe tomorrow—"

"Tomorrow? What about right now?"

"But—"

"You just sit right there."

"Sam—"

"This time, I'll get it right, you'll see." He rose, backing away several feet. As he looked through the viewfinder to frame the shot, however, he saw that Lucky was unbuttoning the collar of her shirt. Slowly and deliberately she smoothed the edges aside, revealing a tantalizing amount of soft, creamy flesh.

Sam lifted his eyes and tried not to gape. "What are you doing?"

Lucky reclined upon the pillows. "Just trying to add a little interest."

"You get any more interesting," Sam growled, "and you'll fog up the lens."

"Don't worry." Her tongue rubbed slowly over her moist pink lips. "I'll be happy to clean it for you."

"Is that an invitation?"

"Guess."

Carefully Sam laid the camera down on the table. "I'll get back to you later," he said and heard Lucky chuckle.

"Don't bet on it," she said and drew him into her arms.

TWO MORNINGS LATER Lucky was sitting in her office humming merrily as she worked. Her mail, just delivered, contained the usual assortment of offerings, including a flyer that touted a new software package for small business management. She started to toss it out, then paused, her thoughts drifting back to Dewey Phillips.

Had he been successful in marketing his own software design? And, more importantly, had the money he'd realized from the sale of the Thunderbird aided his mother's recovery? As to the T-Bird itself, Lucky knew that Clem had had it in the back bay all the previous week, but somehow she'd missed seeing the end result.

Pleased to have an excuse to get out from behind her desk, she sauntered out to the garage. Clem was there, poking at the underbelly of a jeep that had been raised up on the lift. At the sound of her voice he turned, wiping grease-stained hands down the front of his work overalls.

"Suspension's shot," he said.

Lucky took in the mechanic's mournful expression. "Can you fix it?"

"Anything can be fixed, but it's not gonna come cheap."

Lucky shrugged. She'd learned long ago not to argue with the inevitable. "Did you finish working on the T-Bird you had back here last week?"

"Sure did." Clem shifted a large wad of gum from one side of his mouth to the other.

"Where is it?"

"Over at Donahue Motors. Helmut's doing some touch-up work on the paint."

Lucky nodded, considering. "Did you get it running okay?"

"That baby ran when it came in," Clem said with satisfaction. "Now it purrs."

She might as well walk over and have a look, Lucky decided. The lot was quiet, and besides it was nice to have an excuse to stop in and say hello to Sam. As she made the long walk down the road, around the end of the fence and back up, her eyes scanned the rows of neatly parked cars. Over on one side, she spotted a Jaguar and a Porsche, both co-owned and both in the process of being restored. The T-Bird, however, was nowhere to be seen.

Lucky entered Donahue Motors' showroom, waved to Joe and walked straight to Sam's office. He was on the phone when she arrived, but he smiled, motioned her to a chair and quickly concluded his conversation. "I've come about the Thunderbird," Lucky said, when he'd turned his attention her way.

"What about it?"

"Clem told me it was over here for some touch-up work, and I just wanted to see how everything turned out."

"Beautifully," said Sam. "That car was a real gem."

"Was?"

Sam nodded, looking pleased. "I didn't say anything because I wanted it to be a surprise. A couple was here twice over the weekend. They test drove the car Sunday, then came back and bought it this morning."

"They... *What?*"

"Bought the car this morning," Sam repeated, at a loss as to how to interpret her unexpected reaction. "Is something wrong?"

"Of course something's wrong!" Lucky cried, aghast. "How could you sell that car?"

"I thought that was the whole idea."

"Well yes.... But not with that car!"

Confusion ebbed. Irritation rose to take its place. "Why not?

"I told you all about it at the time..." Lucky gazed at the bewildered expression on Sam's face. Clearly he hadn't the slightest idea what she was talking about. "The car belonged to a man named Dewey Phillips. Remember him?"

Sam searched his memory and came up empty. "No, should I?"

"The night you had the flu and I came over and brought you soup—I told you all about him, about how the car had been in his family for years, but now his mother was sick..." Lucky's voice trailed away lamely. "Doesn't any of this sound familiar to you?"

Slowly Sam shook his head. "The only thing I remember about that night was being nursed by a woman with the hands of a courtesan and the backbone of a drill sergeant. Other than that, I'm pretty foggy."

"Maybe I didn't pick the best time to explain."

"Maybe?"

"All right," Lucky sighed. "In light of what's happened since, make that definitely."

"We're both paying attention now," Sam said gently, still not quite sure why she was so upset. "Why don't you try explaining the whole thing to me again?"

This time when Lucky told the story, she made sure that Sam missed none of the details. Slowly and patiently, she described everything that had happened. "So you can see why I hadn't planned on selling that car," she said at the end.

Sam's fingertip was tracing an idle pattern across the surface of the blotter and he surveyed its progress with a preoccupied frown. "To tell the truth," he admitted finally, "I can't. If you bought the car without intending to sell it, then what you were actually doing was offering the man a secured loan. That's a banker's job, not ours. What you tried to do may have been altruistic, but it wasn't realistic."

"Sure it was." Lucky straightened in her chair. "The whole point of this venture is to make a profit. And we would have on that car, too."

"How?"

"By incorporating the work we'd done into its price, the same way we always do." She glared at Sam in exasperation. "I wasn't planning to *give* the car back, for pete's sake. Nor would I have held on to it indefinitely. But I don't see the harm in letting it sit for a little while until Dewey had a chance to get back on his feet."

"Maybe you can't, but I can. We're dealing with a highly specialized market. Buyers for cars in that price range don't happen along every day. We'd have to be crazy to turn them away purely for the sake of some sort of sentimental speculation."

Lucky's eyes widened. "Sentimental speculation?"

"Come on. You can't seriously tell me that you think the decision made good business sense."

"Maybe not, but it made good human sense."

"Perhaps." Sam's shoulders rose and fell in a weary shrug. "But it's a moot point now. The sale has been made. Even if I wanted to undo it—which I don't—it's too late."

Lucky pushed her chair back, away from Sam's desk, increasing the space between them. It occurred to her that the more they'd talked, the more she'd felt like pulling back, as though the physical distance was a mirror of the emotional gap that suddenly seemed to yawn between them.

Never before had their differences seemed so clear-cut, nor so insurmountable. The conflict that had arisen was more than a business dispute. It was an unwelcome reminder of all the things she tried so hard not to think about whenever she and Sam were together—a reflection of their two, basically incompatible, approaches to life. Lucky wouldn't dream of shortchanging compassion for the sake of the bottom line, while Sam, apparently, saw nothing wrong in doing exactly that.

A lump gathered in the back of Lucky's throat as she looked at Sam and read the lack of comprehension in his eyes. Not only didn't he agree with her about the disposition of the Thunderbird, but he couldn't even seem to understand why she was so upset. And it was that realization, sudden and sharp, that chilled her down to the bone.

It was one thing to convince herself as she had for the past six weeks, that she could live, for now, without the promises that Sam was so reluctant to offer. And it was quite another to confront his skepticism, and even contempt, for the values she held so dear. By telling herself that what she had with Sam was enough, Lucky had been denying a key part of her nature, a part that was vital to her very well-being. There was no room in his life for concepts like family and commitment, and love that endured forever—and for her, there was no life without them.

She needed desperately to get away. She needed time to be alone and to think. Grasping the arms of the chair, she rose quickly.

"I'm sorry we can't seem to agree," she said stiffly.

Sam frowned. He knew Lucky was angry. If her tone hadn't clued him in, the rigid set to her shoulders was a sure giveaway.

All right, so maybe he had thrown a monkey wrench into her plans, but he certainly hadn't done it on purpose. They'd approached the same situation with different sets of values, that's all. He'd be damned if he knew what made her so sure hers were right, and his were wrong. Nevertheless, it was clear that they needed to talk.

"How about dinner?" he asked as Lucky reached the door.

She turned slowly and looked at him, still sitting behind his desk. Her gaze traveled slowly from his rumpled hair to his beautiful gray eyes, to the tantalizing twist in the sexiest mouth she'd ever seen. He was the only man she'd ever loved, perhaps the only man she ever would. And walking away from him was going to be the hardest thing she'd ever done.

"Sorry," she said. "I'm busy."

The door closed behind her with chilling finality.

ON TUESDAY NIGHT, Lucky worked late. Wednesday, she simply unplugged her phone. On Thursday when Sam called, she pleaded lack of sleep—certainly no lie under the circumstances—and turned him down yet again. Sooner or later he'd get the picture, she thought grimly. And she could only hope it was going to be sooner because her willpower couldn't stand much more.

As she wandered around her empty house Friday night, Lucky didn't know which was worse, the pain of losing what they'd had together, or the sorrow for the future that would never be. She realized now that all her hopes, all her dreams, had been built upon nothing more than an empty sham. She'd seen Sam not as he was, but as she wanted him to be.

She'd never lied to herself before, but to keep Sam Donahue in her life she'd made an exception. And she'd never regretted a decision more.

More than once, Sam had warned her, but she had refused to listen. He'd told her he was a loner, yet she'd managed to convince herself that it was a role that had fallen to him by necessity rather than choice. He'd told her he didn't want any commitments, and though she'd accepted his words on the surface, deep down inside, she'd been sure he'd change his mind.

All along, Lucky realized ruefully, she'd been so caught up in her own romantic fantasies about love and living happily ever after that she'd refused to see the reality of the situation until it had jumped up and bitten her. The simple truth of the matter was Sam didn't want family ties, and she couldn't live without them.

When the phone rang on the table beside her, Lucky started. She hadn't heard from Sam in almost twenty-four hours, and though she'd come to dread his calls, one small, insidiously optimistic portion of her psyche couldn't help but feel that as long as he didn't give up, there was still hope.

When she answered the phone, however, the person on the other end of the line was not Sam, but her sister, Isabel.

"I know it's short notice," Isabel said breathlessly. "But Bill's got a client in town who decided to stay over for the weekend. He and his wife have invited us out tonight—it's the sort of thing you don't dare refuse—but I can't find anyone to stay with the twins. Lucky, you don't suppose . . . ?"

Lucky grinned, picturing her sister's rambunctious two-year-olds. Evan and Quinn were a two-man wrecking team, and at the moment they sounded like just what she needed to get her mind off her troubles.

"Sure," she said. "I'd be happy to take them."

"We're going to be very late. . . ."

"No problem. Just bring their pajamas, a couple of changes of clothing, and one of those sidebars I can hook on the bed in the guest bedroom."

"You're sure?" Isabel sounded nothing if not eager to be convinced.

"Positive. You two go out and have a great time, and the twins and I will see you in the morning."

An hour later, Evan and Quinn were ensconced on the couch in the den. Evan was sucking happily on a bottle. Quinn, after pronouncing his brother a baby, was taking his juice from a cup. "You two stay right there, okay?" Lucky cast them a wary glance. "I'm just going to go in the kitchen and heat up some spaghetti for your dinner."

"Don't like 'ghetti," Quinn informed her belligerently.

"What do you like?"

"Grapes."

Lucky's brow furrowed. "Grapes?"

Evan nodded along with his brother. "And Cheerios."

Lucky looked back and forth between them. She didn't have any grapes in the house, or any Cheerios, either. "How about hot dogs?" she tried.

"Yeah!" cried Quinn and his brother seconded the motion. "Hot dogs!"

Lucky was lifting the cooked frankfurters out of boiling water when the doorbell rang. She paused, tongs in one hand, potholder in the other, and was debating what to do when the sound of a loud crash, followed by a piercing wail, made the decision for her. She dropped everything and ran.

As Lucky skidded through the hall, she was vaguely aware of the front door being flung open, of Sam, frowning mightily and sprinting in her direction. There was no time to assimilate the information, however, for the next stride carried her through the open doorway and into the den.

Her first reaction was one of relief. Things didn't look nearly as bad as the scene her vivid imagination had conjured up. Quinn, crying loudly, was sitting on the floor next to the tipped over coffee table, while Evan, seemingly oblivious to his brother's plight, was still engrossed in his cartoon.

Quickly she knelt and gathered the crying child in her arms. "Are you hurt?"

Wordlessly Quinn shook his head.

"Did the table tip over and scare you?"

This time he nodded, his tears already beginning to subside.

"Lucky?"

She looked up and saw Sam standing in the doorway. Her heart, that traitorous organ, leaped straight into her throat. If it hadn't been for the children, she might have been tempted to throw herself into his arms. As it was, she managed a shaky wave.

Sam's eyes, warm with concern, skimmed around the room. "Is everything all right?"

"I think so." Lucky stood, placing Quinn beside his brother on the couch. "I don't see any blood."

"Blood?"

"With these two, you never know."

Sam nodded slowly, taking it all in. "And they are?"

"Evan and Quinn Gilbert. They belong to my sister, Isabel, and her husband, Bill. Actually, for tonight, they belong to me." Lucky knew she was babbling, but was powerless to stop. Because if she stopped talking about the children, then she was going to have to think about other things. Like for starters, what was Sam doing there?

Shoving his hands deep in his pockets, Sam leaned against the doorjamb and prepared to enjoy the show as the boys began to squabble and Lucky stepped between them to mediate. Until that moment, he hadn't been at all sure why he had come. But now, smiling softly as he watched a blond-haired gamine with laughing brown eyes take on two pint-sized hellions, he knew the answer was simple. He'd come because he'd had no other choice.

It didn't take a genius to figure out that Lucky had spent the better part of the last week avoiding him. Prompted by their disagreement over the Thunderbird, she'd gone out of her way to give him plenty of the time and space that had once seemed so important. The problem was, in Lucky's absence, time seemed endless and space was simply one more commodity to fill.

Funny, thought Sam. He was used to spending a good deal of time alone. He'd always thought he preferred things that way. But this past week, for the first time in his life, he'd been not only alone, but lonely. He'd missed Lucky's exuberant presence, felt incomplete in a way he'd never before experienced.

Looking back, it was still incredible to him the way their disagreement over the Thunderbird had gotten so out of hand. In the past they'd at least made a stab at resolving their differences. This time, however, Lucky had refused to give them a chance. So tonight, that was exactly what he meant to do—give them both an opportunity to talk. Not about business, but about themselves.

"I was going to ask you to dinner." Sam glanced ruefully at the twins. "I guess that's probably out?"

Lucky flashed him a cheeky grin. Now that Sam was there, actually standing in her house, she couldn't seem to do much else but grin. "Hardier souls than I have tried to contain these two in public and failed. Of course, if you really want to . . ."

"On second thought, I think I'll pass. What are you serving here?"

"Hot dogs."

Sam's lips twitched. "Hasn't anyone ever told you that the way to a man's heart is through his stomach?"

"You try telling that to a two-year-old."

"I get the picture. Hot dogs it is."

"That's odd," Lucky mused aloud. "I don't recall hearing an invitation."

Sam tried out his hungriest, and most beguiling, smile.

Lucky took a moment to catch her breath as she pretended to consider the idea. There was no reason Sam had to know that her insides had just melted down into her socks. Still, there was something she had to know first.

"Why did you come here tonight, Sam?"

There were a dozen ways he could answer that question. And yet in reality there was only one. He reached out and took Lucky's hand, wrapping his long, strong fingers around hers.

"I came," he said simply, "because I love you."

## 14

OF COURSE AN ANSWER like that was hardly the sort that would get a man thrown out on the street, Lucky mused as she went back to the kitchen and put the finishing touches on their meal. But neither was she ready to break out the champagne. Sam had told her before that he loved her, and much as the declaration warmed her, she also knew that, for them, love meant two very different things.

Then again, if fate wanted to provide her with a co-babysitter in the form of a dynamite gray-eyed hunk, who was she to argue? She'd spent the past five days agonizing, analyzing, and not coming up with a single viable solution. Tonight, she was simply going to sit back and enjoy.

Lucky served the meal at the kitchen table, but owing to the twins' table manners, a good deal of it ended up on the floor.

"How do you have the patience?" Sam marveled as Lucky slipped a hand under the table and picked up the plastic bottle of catsup, yet again.

"Easy." She plopped the bottle back on the table and re-tucked Quinn's napkin firmly in the neck of his shirt. "I just keep telling myself that it's only for a couple of hours and tomorrow this time, they'll be Isabel's problem."

"What about when you have children of your own? Then they'll be your problem twenty-four hours a day."

"Only if I choose to look at it that way, and believe me, I've never met a mother who did. Besides," Lucky added, deliberately busying herself with adjusting Evan's seat, "I know you think of me as wildly impetuous, but in some ways, I'm very old-fashioned. By the time I have a child, I'll also have a husband, and we'll share the role of parenting together."

Well that put him back in his place, thought Sam. No doubt it had been intended to accomplish just that very thing. Lucky was making plans for her future, but she obviously wasn't under any illusions as to whether or not they included him.

Whose fault was that? Sam asked himself irritably. He was the one who'd been holding back, the one who'd insisted on taking things slow. How was Lucky supposed to know where they were going, when he wasn't even sure himself?

Shoving another bite of hot dog in his mouth, Sam chewed slowly as an image of Lucky floated into his thoughts. She was holding a baby in her arms, pressing its smooth cheek to hers and crooning softly. Abruptly, a shaft of jealousy, hot and sharp, cut through him at the possibility that the child might not be his.

He'd never thought of himself as fatherhood material. But then again, he'd always doubted that he'd ever truly fall in love. And he was in love with Lucky Vanderholden, there was no question about that. Slowly but surely, she'd opened his heart, and his mind, to a wealth of new emotion and a host of new possibilities.

Every day, the joy he found in their relationship seemed to deepen. Every day, the silken threads that bound them together seemed that much more secure. Once he'd been daunted by the very thought of promises that were meant to last a lifetime; now all at once, the idea of living without them seemed impossible.

With a sudden start of revelation, Sam realized that in his heart the commitment he'd thought he'd been shying away from had already taken place. The only thing he hadn't done was say the words.

"Did I warn you that you were going to work for your supper?"

Roused from his thoughts, Sam looked up to find Lucky watching him intently from across the table. There were things he wanted to say to her, important things that had already waited much too long. But one look at the two pairs of curious eyes on either side of them, and he knew he was going to have to wait a little longer.

"As a matter of fact, no," he replied.

"Pity." Lucky shrugged, but her eyes were dancing wickedly.

"What did you have in mind?"

She lifted Evan from his chair, then followed quickly with Quinn. Of one mind, the boys raced out of the kitchen, yelling happily. "You have a choice. Either kitchen detail..." Lucky smiled, feeling quite certain she knew which chore he would choose. "Or else you can go in and round up those two wild Indians and get them started on their bath."

He was an old hand in the kitchen. Judging from the number of frozen dinners he'd seen in her freezer, perhaps even more experienced that Lucky herself. The clean-up would be a breeze. Which is why he was as surprised as anyone when he heard himself say, "By now you probably need a break. Why don't you work in here while I take those two upstairs?"

It was a good thing Lucky was already sitting down, otherwise she just might have ended up on the floor. As it was she remained seated and stared after him, feeling utterly dumbfounded, as Sam left the room. Even then, she didn't move, waiting instead for the inevitable screams of protest that would send her flying to Sam's aid.

When five minutes passed and none came, Lucky didn't know whether to be disgruntled or relieved. Sticking her head out into the hall, she saw that the den was empty, then heard the unmistakable sounds of running water and delighted giggling coming from upstairs.

It had to be a trick, Lucky decided. Craning her head around she looked up to the landing. "Sam? Is everything all right?"

His response floated serenely down the stairway. "Just fine."

Shaking her head and muttering under her breath, Lucky did the only thing she could under the circumstances. She marched back into the kitchen and did the dishes.

He'd never have guessed that two children, and such small ones at that, could be so adept at maritime maneuvers, thought Sam. Deprived of their usual toys, the twins had converted everything from shampoo bottles to soap dishes into impromptu battleships. Now, with a minimum of washing and a maximum of splashing, they were engaged in a no-holds-barred war for supremacy of the tub.

Kneeling beside the tub, Sam reached into the water, plowing his hand through a mountain of bubbles in an effort to retrieve the soap. Slick and slimy, it slipped from his grasp and shot between Evan's legs. With a sigh, Sam gave it up as lost. They might not get perfectly clean, but at least they seemed to be wearing themselves out.

The merit of his plan became obvious ten minutes later as the children's energy level began to wind down. By that time Sam's shirt was dripping wet and a spray of bubbles decorated the top of his head. He flipped the plug to let the water drain out, then lifted the twins, one by one, and wrapped them in thick, terry cloth towels.

Lucky arrived on the scene just in time to take Evan while Sam lifted Quinn into his arms. Thumb in his mouth, the two-year-old nestled his head against Sam's shoulder. With a warm feeling deep inside, Sam snuggled him closer, marveling at the ease with which the boy displayed his emotions.

Had he ever been that free with his feelings? Sam wondered. Had he ever, even at Quinn's age, been so certain of his acceptance that he could give his trust without reservation? Trust was what it all came down to. Even after he'd realized he was falling in love with Lucky, he'd still been wary—not because he was afraid to trust her, but because he didn't dare trust himself.

For as long as he could remember, he'd lived by his intellect, and it had always seemed enough. Only recently had he begun to realize that there were things rational thought couldn't begin to define. There was no logic to caring, no ready answer to explain the way he felt with Lucky by his side. He'd shied away from love because he'd known all along that it was the one gamble he couldn't afford to lose.

But now, with Lucky in his life, the possibilities seemed limitless. And as soon as the twins were safely taken care of, he had every intention of telling her how he felt.

Tired from their exertion, the boys made no protest as Sam and Lucky bundled them into their pajamas and tucked them into bed. As the two adults tiptoed out into the hall and pulled the door shut behind them, the children were already well on their way to being asleep.

"Whew," said Sam.

"My sentiments exactly." Lucky flicked an amused finger over his wet shirt. "Have fun in the bath?"

"Not nearly as much as I'm about to have."

Was it a trick of the light, she wondered, or had Sam's eyes suddenly gone all dark and smoky? Her fingers clutched at the sodden material of his shirt, feeling the hard lines of his chest beneath. Desire, hot and sweet, melted through her.

"Maybe we ought to start by getting you out of these wet clothes," she said huskily.

Sam's mouth moved down to nuzzle the lobe of Lucky's ear. "I like a woman with a practical streak."

"And here I thought all along that it was my body you couldn't resist."

"That, too," Sam murmured. He paused then, lifting his head to listen. "What about the twins?"

"Don't worry." Lucky took Sam's hand in hers and led him toward her bedroom. "Once you finally get them settled, they're in for the night."

"Sounds perfect."

Lucky glanced up and smiled softly. "I thought so."

In the four days since she and Sam had last been together, she'd never stopped missing him. Now, as they came to a halt beside the bed, she went into his arms as naturally as if they'd never been apart. Sam's hands circled her waist, pressing against the small of her back as he pulled her close.

Then his mouth was on hers, hard and hungry, as Lucky rose up on her toes to meet him. His tongue slid between her parted lips and she drew it to her, sucking him deep into her mouth and surrounding him with her warmth. A moan drifted between them, and Lucky recognized it as her own. Her senses were swamped with pleasure; the reeling of her head was a glorious sensation.

She drew a deep, quivering breath and her breasts lifted, grazing the hard muscles of his chest. As if the clothing between them didn't exist, she felt the tangle of crisp hairs that curled beneath his shirt teasing her sensitive skin. Immediately her nipples hardened in response, jutting forward as Sam reached up to cup the weight of her breast in his palm.

"Oh how I've missed you," Lucky said with a sigh. Her hands clutched him to her, holding as though she would never let him go.

"I'm here," Sam murmured. "I'm here, Lucky, for just as long as you want me."

Lucky's eyelids fluttered shut as his mouth lowered to hers once more. Gently he tasted the sweetness of her lips. Slowly his tongue traced their outline. Then his hand came up to cradle the back of her head as his tongue plunged between her lips with a thrust that Lucky felt as a jolt of sensation shimmering throughout her entire body.

Bracing back against him, she moaned with need. Her body was throbbing, filled with a languid heaviness that left her weak and breathless. Her thighs parted, and Sam slipped his leg between them. He shifted slightly and Lucky felt the hard sinew of his hips grind against her own. When he began to rub slowly back and forth, the ache inside her centered, finding its pulsating focus deep within her loins.

A soft, whimpering cry was torn from deep within her throat, and Sam smothered the sound with his lips. Never had he known a woman whose passions ignited so quickly, and knowledge of her arousal spurred his own as nothing else could have.

Piece by piece, their clothing fell to the floor, discarded by eager hands, then forgotten. Naked finally, they tumbled to the bed. Sam's head dipped down to nestle between Lucky's breasts, his tongue finding the already swollen nipples and bathing them gently.

His hands slid lower, then lower still across the flat plane of her midriff to the nest of soft curls beneath. Lucky gasped sharply as his fingers found the core of her femininity, stroking until her body felt as taut as a drawn bowstring, until her nerve endings throbbed with unbearable pleasure.

Then she was moving to take control, teasing Sam with her hot breath, tasting him with her hungry mouth until he writhed with impatience beneath her. Pushing him down upon the pillows, Lucky straddled his hips. His fingers grasped her buttocks and guided her to him.

Lucky sighed with pleasure as Sam filled her body with the same exquisite sense of completion as his love had filled her soul. If this was all there was, thought Lucky, if this was all there could ever be, it was enough. Urgently he began to move. The rhythm pushed her harder and faster. Her head arched back as she felt the first wave of sensation rock through her. He cried out her name once, then again, as a storm of consummate pleasure washed over them, overpowering need and will both, until nothing existed save completion.

A long moment passed before Lucky caught her breath. It was longer still before she summoned the energy to lift her head and gaze down into Sam's passion-dark eyes. "That," she said, in a tone tinged with awe, "was incredible."

Sam's hands came up to cup her neck, his fingers gently massaging her nape. "That," he said with satisfaction, "is because you love me."

Lucky chuckled softly. "Pretty sure of yourself, aren't you?"

He couldn't help it if he sounded smug. He *felt* smug. For the first time in his life, he had his priorities straight. Not only did he finally know exactly what he wanted, he also had the incredible good fortune to be holding her in his arms. He was in love with the most wonderful woman in the world, and she was in love with him. They were going to spend the rest of their lives together, in total joy and at least partial harmony. There was only one thing that remained to be said.

"Marry me," Sam proposed.

There were only a limited number of things that could have roused Lucky out of the pleasure-induced lethargy that was beginning to steal over her body. Sam, with unerring accuracy, had found one of them.

"What?"

"I love you, Lucky. And I want you to marry me."

She rolled off Sam's chest and landed on the bed beside him with a thump. "Now?"

"Well no," Sam allowed. "At least not right this minute. I was thinking we might want to put some clothes on first."

An impatient shake of her head sent Lucky's curls dancing. "That isn't what I meant. What I want to know is why you're asking me now."

"This is a bad time?"

Lucky drew a deep breath and sighed. How could she even begin to explain? She'd thought she wanted more than anything to hear Sam say those words. Now that he had, she realized that it was all wrong. She loved Sam, the feelings she had for him were beyond all measure, and it was for precisely that reason that she couldn't help but question his motives.

"I've pressured you into doing this, haven't I?" Lucky asked softly.

Sam's lips drew together in a frown. Somehow things weren't going at all the way he'd expected. "Of course not. Why would you think that?"

"Have you missed me this week, Sam?"

"You know I have." His fingers grasped her chin and tilted her face up to his. "I love you, Lucky, and I love spending time with you."

"You see? That's exactly my point. It's only the fact that we've been apart that's made you start thinking this way. When we were together what you wanted most was your freedom."

"I *thought* I wanted my freedom," Sam corrected gently. "There's a big difference. Six months ago, even two months ago, you'd have been right. Now I know better. I've learned a lot of things since I met you, and one of them is that independence is nothing without someone to share it with." Sam paused, his gray eyes boring down into hers. "I'd like that person to be you."

Miserably, Lucky shifted her gaze away. "I can't."

"Why not?"

"Because then I'd have to live with the knowledge that I'd forced you to change just to suit me. I've been doing a lot of thinking about us, too, and I realized that I was very wrong to want you to be something you weren't. You're a wonderful man, Sam, but—"

"Don't say it," Sam growled. "In fact, don't even think it."

"I'm just trying to stop you from leaping in and doing something impulsive."

"Me?" He shot her a look. "You know perfectly well I've never done anything impulsive in my entire life."

"All the more reason not to start now."

It took work to keep her voice calm, but with effort Lucky managed it. She had no other choice. If she slipped up now, if she allowed so much as one small chink in the wall she was erecting between them, she was horribly afraid that Sam might wind up doing something he'd regret for the rest of his life.

Abruptly Sam sat up, bracing his back against the hard headboard. His patience was fading rapidly. "Just what makes you think," he demanded, "that this proposal of mine is so rash and ill-considered?"

"Isn't it?"

"Of course not."

Lucky swung over onto her stomach, braced her elbows on the bed and set her chin in her hands. "Then when you came here tonight, you were planning all along to propose?"

"Well no, not exactly."

Lucky's eloquent silence spoke for itself.

"What I was planning was for us to talk. What I was hoping was that we'd wind up in bed."

"And what you didn't expect," Lucky finished for him, "was that you'd be leaving in the morning with a lifetime commitment. Damn it, Sam!" Lucky's balled up fist struck the mattress in frustration. "I know you and I love you, and there isn't an impetuous bone in your entire body!"

He'd just defended one side of the argument, now Sam found himself backing the other. "What about the way I jumped right into our joint venture?"

"That's different, you're enough of a businessman to recognize a good deal when you hear one."

"I rest my case."

Lucky glared at him in exasperation. "Our relationship is not a business deal, Sam. And I flatly refuse to let you leap now and look later."

"Don't I have anything to say about that?"

Stubbornly she shook her head. "I think you ought to retract your proposal—"

"The proposal stands."

"Until you've had more time to think," Lucky finished firmly.

Sam's laugh held little humor. "Shall we synchronize our watches?"

"That won't be necessary."

"Thank God." Muttering under his breath, Sam slid back down onto the bed. His fist punched the pillow several times before he tucked it under his head, turned on his side facing the other way, then promptly fell asleep.

Which was probably just exactly what she deserved, Lucky decided miserably. The things she'd said hadn't been pleasant, but it had had to be done. If Sam really wanted to marry her, if he was truly committed to the idea of their spending a lifetime together, then he never would have let her talk him out of the idea. That she'd been able to do so only proved that she knew what she was doing.

Damn it, thought Lucky, she really hated being right.

WHEN SAM AWOKE the next morning, bright ribbons of sunlight streamed across the bed. A glance at the clock confirmed that it was after eight, which wasn't surprising, considering he'd spent most of the night pretending to be asleep, rather than actually managing the feat itself.

Though her side of the bed was still warm, her pillow fragrant with the scent of her hair, Lucky herself was gone. Judging by the amount of noise coming from downstairs, she was feeding the twins breakfast. Sam considered pulling on a pair of pants and going down to join them, then quickly changed his mind.

She'd really thrown him a curve last night. This morning when he faced her, he wanted to be fully awake, alert, and dressed. He was going to look every inch the solid, upstanding citizen he'd always thought himself to be. Then, when he repeated his proposal of marriage, she'd have no option but to take him seriously.

Fifteen minutes later, Sam was showered, shaved and ready to take on the world. As he started down the stairs, he realized that the decibel level had dropped dramatically. Now the hum of voices coming from the kitchen was subdued, suggesting adult conversation rather than the excited chatter of two toddlers. When he reached the bottom and turned the corner, he saw why.

"Morning," Bill said affably. If he was at all surprised to see Sam come ambling into Lucky's kitchen, freshly showered and shaved, his expression didn't show it. "I just stopped by to pick up the twins. I see you two both managed to survive."

"We enjoyed ourselves," Sam said sincerely. He walked over to the counter and poured himself a cup of coffee. "Your sons are a delight."

"Sometimes," Bill conceded with a grin as he rose. "I'd better be going. As soon as I drop the kids off at home, Frank and Hal and I are going to go fishing. Weather's perfect—with any luck, we'll catch dinner." He started toward the den, then paused, turning back. "Say Sam, why don't you join us?"

"Me?" Sam looked up in surprise. "I've never been fishing."

"You know what they say—no time like the present."

Actually that wasn't what Lucky had said the night before when he'd decided to try something different. No, as he recalled, she'd said if he hadn't been an impetuous person before, he had no reason to start now. So she didn't think he had an impulsive bone in his entire body, did she? Well he'd just see about that!

"Sure," said Sam, his grin slow and easy. "I think I'd like that."

Lucky choked on a sip of coffee. "You would?"

His grin widened at Lucky's startled expression. "Why not?" he asked as Bill ducked out to retrieve the twins. "You know me, spontaneity is my middle name."

"Sam, you don't know what you're getting into. My brothers are hard-core fishermen. When they go out on the lake, they're gone for hours."

"Sounds perfect," Sam said affably. "Who knows? Maybe I'll catch dinner."

"Maybe you'll fall in the lake and catch pneumonia."

"Tsk, tsk, tsk. Just last night, you were trying to give me my freedom. And now you want to take it back?"

"Of course not, it's just that . . ."

"Yes?"

Could she help it if she didn't have an answer to that? "It's your life," Lucky conceded finally. "I guess you're old enough to know what you're doing."

"You're right," Sam replied, suddenly serious. "Think about it." He leaned down and brushed a quick kiss across her lips, then he followed Bill and the twins out the door.

Lucky did think about what Sam had said. All day long as she worked at the lot, her thoughts whirled endlessly. Certainly Sam was old enough—more than old enough—to make his own decision. And she had neither the right nor, under the circumstances, the desire to make them for him.

Once again, Lucky realized, she'd been guilty of trying to make Sam change. And once again she'd been wrong. If he was truly convinced that he wanted to marry her, she'd have to be crazy to send him away. And as soon as he returned, she'd tell him exactly that.

For some reason she'd assumed Sam would stop by when he got back. At the very least, she expected him to call. But by six o'clock she was ready to close the lot, and she still hadn't heard a thing.

Lucky stared at the phone on her desk for several long minutes before finally pulling the instrument toward her and dialing. A quick conversation with Frank told her everything she hadn't wanted to hear. Sam had been back for hours. Although her brothers had spent the whole day on the lake, Sam had remained with them only until after lunch. Frank hadn't seen him since early afternoon and had no idea where he'd gone.

Lucky slammed down the receiver, frowning irritably. It was one thing to hand a man his freedom, and another entirely to have him take it!

She worried all the way home, and once there, only felt worse. Everywhere she walked in the small house, she felt Sam's presence. The den brought back memories of their first date. The kitchen reminded her of meals they'd cooked, and the vibrant, laughing conversations they'd shared while eating them. And her bedroom . . . The scenes it brought to mind were enough to make her blush.

Was it possible that Sam could have taken her advice about reconsidering his proposal? Lucky wondered as another hour dragged by. If so, she'd just made the biggest mistake of her entire life. She was the one who had sent him away. How would she ever fill the hole he'd leave in her life if he decided not to return?

The sound of a car horn, low and melodic, brought Lucky to her feet. Maybe it was only wishful thinking, but she had to see what kind of automobile had produced such beautiful music. She'd never heard Sam's horn after all. Maybe . . .

Striding purposely through the front hall, Lucky flung open the door—and walked straight into Sam's arms.

"Well this is a pleasant surprise," he said with a grin. "I was hoping you'd be glad to see me, but I hadn't counted on a greeting like this."

"You're here," Lucky said inanely. Her hands ran up Sam's arms and over his shoulders. Now that he was there, she felt an incredible urge to touch every inch of him, to convince herself that he really had returned. "Come on inside."

"In a minute."

Sam's eyes were dancing. Any minute now he was going to flash that lopsided grin and then, by God, she'd drag him in....

"I have something to show you."

"What?" Lucky craned her head around to look over his shoulder, but Sam held up a hand to block her view.

"Not yet. First I have something to ask you."

"The answer's yes," Lucky replied without hesitation.

"It isn't a yes or no question."

"Oh." With effort, she hid her disappointment. "Okay then, shoot."

"How do you feel about nontraditional wedding presents?"

She shot him a quizzical look. "You mean like cuckoo clocks instead of toasters?"

"Not exactly."

"Sam Donahue," Lucky fumed, "if you don't tell me what's going on right this very moment, I'm going to punch you!"

"I believe you mean that."

"You better believe it! If there's one thing growing up with four brothers taught me, it's a mean right hook."

"Hold the hook," Sam said with a chuckle. "If you still want to use it after we talk, you can take your best shot." He led her to the wooden swing on the side of the porch. There was just enough room for them both to sit if they didn't mind being close. Snuggled hip to hip and thigh to thigh, neither minded a bit. The swing dipped gently then began to rock back and forth.

"I haven't had many important relationships in my life," Sam said slowly. "Perhaps that's my own fault. As a child, I was encouraged to excel, not relate. As I grew up I became a whiz at projecting long-range plans and setting goals that would keep me busy for years to come. I was so successful at orchestrating my life that I had myself convinced the satisfaction I derived from that was enough.

"And then," said Sam, gazing deep into Lucky's eyes. "I met you. You turned my life upside down, and inside out, and I began to realize that nothing was ever going to be the same again. While I was busy telling myself that I'd feel smothered in a family the size of yours, your relatives were equally busy showing me just how much love and caring I'd missed out on in my own life."

"The fishing trip," Lucky said with a gulp as a sudden thought struck her. "My brothers didn't . . ."

"They did."

"Oh."

"Don't sound so glum," Sam consoled her. "Actually I rather enjoyed listening to your brothers extol your virtues. And then there was Bill, who provided the in-law's point of view."

Lucky sighed audibly. "I may as well hear it all."

"He said," Sam informed her with a grin, "that it only takes a month or two to get your breath back. After that, being surrounded by Vanderholdens can actually be quite pleasant."

"With a glowing recommendation like that, I can see why you didn't rush right back this afternoon."

"Actually that had nothing to do with it. As it happens I had some business to attend to."

Lucky's brow rose. "I thought you didn't work Saturdays."

"Call it personal business."

Lucky's eyes narrowed as she remembered his earlier question. Before good sense could stop her, she blurted out, "You bought me a wedding present!" She laughed then, whooping with delight as she saw by the expression on Sam's face that she'd been right.

"Damn it," he growled. "There you go jumping ahead again. This was supposed to be a surprise."

"Sorry," Lucky said contritely. Now that she knew for sure which way things were headed, she had all the time in the world. "Go ahead, surprise me."

Instead of answering, Sam rose and brought her up with him. They walked down the small flight of steps at the front of the house, then Sam led the way to the driveway on the side. There, parked in the shade of the garage, sat Dewey Phillips's Thunderbird.

"Where did that come from?" Lucky gasped.

"I bought it back," Sam said with satisfaction. The keys dangled from his upraised hand. "It took some doing, but this afternoon I finally managed to convince the people who'd bought the car to sell it to me. It's all yours now, to do whatever you want with."

Lucky ran her fingers over the smooth hood. Her voice when she spoke was soft, tremulous. "Would you mind terribly if I wanted to sell it?"

"Not at all. Actually I think I'd be a little disappointed if you said anything else."

Lucky smiled at his response, but she knew there was one more question that needed to be asked. "Why did you do it?"

"Why?" Sam echoed blankly.

"I mean," Lucky said slowly, "did you do it just to humor me, or was there something more?"

Sam thought for a long moment before answering. "A bit of both," he said finally. "I have to admit I still don't fully understand the way you felt about the deal you made. Nor do I necessarily agree. On the other hand," he added, drawing her into his arms, "all that means is that you've got the rest of your life to explain it to me. Who knows, maybe when I finally have a real family of my own . . ."

Lucky raised up on her toes and touched her lips to his. Love rose and swelled within her until she was so filled with the emotion that she couldn't speak. Instead she simply sighed with happiness as Sam covered her mouth with his. The kiss they shared was slow and warm, and affirmation of the blissful intensity of the feelings they shared.

After a long moment, Lucky pulled reluctantly away. "Sam?"

"Hmm?"

"Is that car really my *wedding present*?"

"That's the deal. You have to say yes, otherwise—"

"You'll save it for your next fiancée?"

Sam choked on a laugh. She wasn't going to make his life easy. Then again, it would never be dull. "Otherwise," he said, "I'll just have to come up with a stronger incentive."

"Like love and caring and the desire to spend the rest of our lives together?"

"Those will do for a start."

"For a start and a finish and everything in between."

"You see?" Sam said as he lowered his mouth once more to hers. "I told you some day we'd learn how to agree."

Coming in June...

# PENNY JORDAN

## a reason for being

We invite you to join us in celebrating Harlequin's 40th Anniversary with this very special book we selected to publish worldwide.

While you read this story, millions of women in 100 countries will be reading it, too.

*A Reason for Being* by Penny Jordan is being published in June in the Presents series in 19 languages around the world. Join women around the world in helping us to celebrate 40 years of romance.

Penny Jordan's *A Reason for Being* is Presents June title #1180. Look for it wherever paperbacks are sold.

HARLEQUIN
*Temptation*

# COMING NEXT MONTH

### #257 DADDY, DARLING Glenda Sanders

Dory Karol and Scott Rowland had the perfect long-distance relationship—until Dory became pregnant. The prospect of parenthood should have brought them closer—both physically and emotionally. But Scott was a reluctant daddy, and it was up to Dory to make them a *loving* family....

### #258 FACE TO FACE Julie Meyers

Griffon Falconer was terribly fond of his beard, and the sexy radio personality wasn't about to give it up. Yet that was exactly what Caiti Kelly was asking him to do. Of course, it was for charity.... In the end, when it came to a contest between his beloved beard and the charming persuasion of Caiti, one would be the winner by a close shave!

### #259 STUCK ON YOU Kristine Rolofson

When wallpaper contractor Maggie McGuire was hired to redecorate Sam Winslow's mansion, she found his two small girls a delightful distraction. Their father, however, was just plain distracting! Maggie and Sam's immediate and undeniable attraction had all the makings of a sticky situation!

### #260 THE HOME STRETCH Karen Percy

Dan Faraday was just the man for Cassie McLean. Pinetop's newest veterinarian loved horses, the small-town life . . . and Cassie. But Dan was only passing through. And Cassie had one rule for her man: he had to know how to stay put....

# Your favorite stories with a brand-new look!!

# *Harlequin American Romance*

---

**Romances that go one step farther...**
**American Romance**

Realistic stories involving people you can relate to and care about.

Compelling relationships between the mature men and women of today's world.

Romances that capture the core of genuine emotions between a man and a woman.

Join us each month for four new titles wherever paperback books are sold.
Enter the world of American Romance.

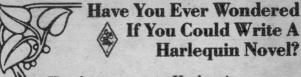

# Have You Ever Wondered If You Could Write A Harlequin Novel?

Here's great news—Harlequin is offering a series of cassette tapes to help you do just that. Written by Harlequin editors, these tapes give practical advice on how to make your characters—and your story—come alive. There's a tape for each contemporary romance series Harlequin publishes.

**Mail order only**

**All sales final**

---